A TIME LORD FOR CHANGE

A collection of drabbles

EDITED by ELTON TOWNEND JONES

COMMISSIONING EDITOR: CLIFF CHAPMAN

With ELTON TOWNEND JONES and BARNABY EATON-JONES

ILLUSTRATED BY GARY ANDREWS

A Time Lord for Change

Copyright © 2016 Chinbeard Books. All rights reserved

First paperback edition printed 2016

No part of this book shall be reproduced or transmitted in any form or by any means, electronic or mechanical, including photocopying, recording or by any information retrieval system without written permission of the author.

Published by Chinbeard Books

Designed and set by Nicholas Hollands

Although every precaution has been taken in the preparation of this book, the publisher and author assume no responsibility for errors of omissions. Neither is any liability assimed for damages resulting in the use of the information contained herein.

All royalties from this book are going to MIND - the Mental Health charity in the UK.

Back cover drabble by John Davies

Interior artwork by Gary Andrews

Cover by Steve Horry

INTRODUCTION

By Cliff Chapman

The thing about depression and anxiety is that it makes life really hard to do. I mean, you might think 'not doing stuff' is just being lazy, but imagine getting breathing trouble and chest pains the minute you wake up. Imagine not doing something not because you can't be bothered, but because of what *Doctor Who* script editor Robert Holmes called the mind's 'spiralling descent syndrome'. You visualise something you have to do not going that well. And then it goes very badly. And then awfully. And you end up a social pariah. So you just can't do it. It's not laziness, or writer's block, or wilful badness – it's a state of mind you cannot control. You really can't. Yes, the people who don't understand say that you can, but that's nonsense. They might not have 'been there before', but sadly they probably have, and 'just being positive' didn't help them either...

Another thing about depression is that it stops you enjoying things you normally love, and sometimes that means not being able to enjoy the magical things this book is all about, like watching *Doctor Who* or writing stuff. And *Doctor Who* is magical. There's something about the flabbiest, CSO-stuffed Pertwee story or even a boisterous, continuity-confused mid-Eighties Sawardfest that feels like a comforting blanket to a certain kind of person. A person like me. And possibly you. (Switch your eras of the series to taste). The magical thing about *Doctor Who*, for people like us, is that it's *there*, and it's a happy thing that distracts, amuses; lets us escape...

The magical thing about writing stuff, is that it has exactly the same effect on us as *Doctor Who* – but sometimes it's hard to get going; it's impossible to imagine filling that big white page with any writing at all, let alone *good* writing...

So. When you've not written anything for weeks, or months, or years, but you want so very, very badly to justify the claim that you write... Well, try a drabble.

A drabble is a small but perfectly-formed creative work of 100 words exactly. Drabbles are brief but marvellous; short, but vivid. Most of the best ideas come like flash fiction, a bit of procrastination to keep you busy but stop you doing other things. And with depression, although one can give no real advice, it's worth saying that achieving tiny, incremental goals can boost confidence and get you moving, doing and smiling again.

Everything you'll read in this book is by *Doctor Who* fans; some of them are more well-known than others, but all of them are wonderful, talented, generous, clever, and creative. Each writer has a working understanding of what *Doctor Who* is, and every one of them has enjoyed playing in the *Doctor Who* sandpit, employing a vast and delightful array of styles (some farce, some slapstick, some dryly witty, some adventurous, some terrifying, some literary, some deep, some timey-wimey, some musical, some lyrical, some utterly mad...).

Nothing in this book is canon. We're unauthorised and unofficial and for charity, but believe what you like when you read these preludes, codas, interludes, character studies, retellings, pastiches, documentary archive ephemera and adventures. This is a book about variety, because *Doctor Who* is about variety. I never give advice, but I will say this: if ever you're depressed, variety will ease that depression... And that sharing things with people who understand helps... Oh, and that this is probably going to be a *brilliant* book to take with you when you go to the loo.

Variety, writing, and *Doctor Who*.

INTRODUCTION (in 100 words)

By Elton Townend Jones

(Clears throat)

Diddley-dum, diddley-dum,
Diddley-diddley, diddley-dum;
Diddley-dum, diddley-dum,
Diddley-diddley, diddley dum;

Diddley-dum, diddley-dum,
Diddley-diddley, diddley-dum;
Diddley-dum, diddley-dum,
Diddley-diddley-
Ooooh-waah-oooooh;
Waaaah-oooh!
Ooh-wah-ooh-wee-ooh-wee-ooh-ee-oo
(Ooh-ee-oo)

Diddley-dum, diddley-dum,
Diddley-diddley, diddley-dum;
Diddley-dum, diddley-dum,
Diddley-diddley, diddley dum;

Ooooh-waah-oooooh;
Waaaah-oooh!
Ooh-wah-ooh-wee-ooh-wee-ooh-ee-oo
(Ooh-ee-oo)

Diddley-dum, diddley-dum,
Diddley-diddley, diddley-dum;
Diddley-dum, diddley-dum,
Diddley-diddley-diddley dum;

Ooh.
Ooh-wee-ooh-wee-ooh;
Ooh-wooh-widdle-woo,
Ooh-wooh-widdle-woo,
Ooh-ooh.

Ooh.

Widdle woo. (Or Plinky-plink!)

Widdle-woo!

Diddley-dum, diddley-dum,
Diddley-diddley, diddley-dum;
Diddley-dum, diddley-dum,
Diddley-diddley-diddley dum;

Ooooh-waah-oooooh;
Waaaah-oooh!

Diddley-dum, diddley-dum,
Diddley-diddley-
Ooooh-waah-oooooh;
Waaaah-oooh!
Diddley-dum, diddley-dum,
BZZZSSSSHHHHEEEEBZZZSSSSHHHHEEEEEEBBZSHHHH!

'Scuse my voice, Delia, but it ought to go *something* like that, I reckon. Now run along, sweetheart, and knock it into shape with your tapes and what-not...

CONTENTS AND CONTRIBUTORS

THE FIRST DOCTOR

By Cliff Chapman, Nigel Peever, Simon Brett, Steve Herbert, Elliot Thorpe, Alan Taylor, Simon A Forward, Lee Ravitz, David Guest, Elton Townend Jones, Tony Eccles, Ilse A Ras, Simon Bucher-Jones, Clive Greenwood, Andrew Mark Thompson, Nick Griffiths, Dan Milco, Robert Simpson, John Isles, Ian Potter, Alan Stevens, Brendan Jones, Brad Wolfe, Kenneth Shinn, Mark Trevor Owen, Matt Barber, Niall Boyce, and Stephen Aintree

THE SECOND DOCTOR

By Simon Bucher-Jones, Mike Watkins, Ash Stewart, Sarah Di-Bella, Alan Stevens, Lee Ravitz, Cliff Chapman, Sam Stone, Nigel Peever, Daniel Wealands, Simon A Forward, John Davies, Alan Graham, Craig Fisher, Elton Townend Jones, Ilse A Ras, David J Howe, Shaqui Le Vesconte, and Jane Sherwin

THE THIRD DOCTOR

By Jon Dear, Simon A Forward, Alan Stevens, Barry James Collins, Robert Simpson, Kenneth Shinn, Lee Rawlings, Brad Wolfe, Tim Gambrell, Shaqui Le Vesconte, JR Loflin, Katy Manning, Richard Barnes, JR Southall, Nigel Peever, Dan Milco, Joanne Harris, Elton Townend Jones, Alan G McWhan, Stephen Mellor, Craig Fisher, and Elliot Thorpe

THE FOURTH DOCTOR

By Paul Driscoll, Simon A Forward, Callum Stewart, Nigel Peever, Simon Bucher-Jones, Lee Rawlings, Ian Baldwin, Dan Milco, David Guest, Cliff Chapman, John Dorney, Mark Trevor Owen, Colleen Hawkins, Matt Barber, Alan G McWhan, Alan Stevens, Paul Magrs, Barnaby Eaton-Jones, Stephen Aintree, Jon Arnold, Danou M. Duifhuizen, Tim Gambrell, Paul Ebbs, Elliot Thorpe, Nick Mellish, Simon Nicholas Kemp, Ash Stewart, Will Ingram, Georgia Ingram, Craig Moss, Fiona Moore, and Brendan Jones

THE FIFTH DOCTOR

By Ilse A Ras, Stephen Aintree, Alan Taylor, Lee Ravitz, JR Southall, Barry James Collins, Neil Perryman, Robert Simpson, Mark Trevor Owen, James Gent, Nigel Peever, Barnaby Eaton-Jones, Matt Barber, Kenneth Shinn, Andrew Bloor, Christine Grit, and Andrew Lawston

THE SIXTH DOCTOR

By Callum Stewart, Terry Molloy, Alan Taylor, James Gent, Lee Ravitz, John Gerard Hughes, Alan G McWhan, Craig Fisher, Ian Ham, Ron Brunwin, and Colin Baker

THE SEVENTH DOCTOR

By Matt Barber, Simon Nicholas Kemp, John Gerard Hughes, Alan Taylor, John Davies, Gareth Alexander, Tim Gambrell, Ian Kubiak, Steve Horry, Andrew Lawston, and Andrew Cartmel

THE EIGHTH DOCTOR

By Craig Fisher and Gareth Kearns

THE WAR DOCTOR

By John Davies with Elton Townend Jones

THE NINTH DOCTOR

By Alan G McWhan, Liam Hogan, Lee Rawlings, Jon Arnold, Robert Shearman, Mark Trevor Owen, Simon Bucher-Jones, Rebecca Vaughan, Douglas M Devaney, and Elton Townend Jones

THE TENTH DOCTOR

By Yasmin Dibella-Back, Piers Beckley, Peter Muscutt, Elliot Thorpe, Craig Fisher, Robin G Burchill, Ian Ham, Gareth Kearns, Lisa T Downey-Dent, Dan Milco, Andrew Bloor, Alan Taylor, Cliff Chapman, Gemma Fraser, Tessa North, JR Southall, Sami Kelsh, Barnaby Eaton-Jones, Barry James Collins, Lou Marie Kerr, Jon Arnold, Liam Hogan, Will Ingram, John Gerard Hughes, Ilse A Ras, Alan G McWhan, John Davies, Simon Brett, Daniel Wealands, Tony Eccles, and Rachel Redhead

THE ELEVENTH DOCTOR

By Daniel Wealands, Gemma Fraser, JR Southall, Alan G McWhan, Christine Grit, Nick Griffiths, Lisa T Downey-Dent, Joy-Amy Wigman, Georgia Ingram, Stephen Aintree, Richard Barnes, Catherine Crosswell, Dan Milco, Simon Brett, Aryldi Moss-Burke, Paul Driscoll, Callum Stewart, Rachel Redhead, JR Loflin, Hendryk Korzeniowski, Alan P Jack, Alan Graham, Verity Smith, Mark Blayney, Lee Rawlings, Penny Andrews, Will Ingram, Simon A Forward, Colleen Hawkins, Simon Nicholas Kemp, Steve Taylor-Bryant, Tim Gambrell, John Davies, Jon Arnold, and Elliot Thorpe

THE TWELFTH DOCTOR

By Paul Ebbs, David Guest, Tessa North, Rob Stradling, Helen Oakleigh, John Davies, Alan Taylor, Nick Mellish, Aryldi Moss-Burke, Penny Andrews, JR Southall, Lisa Wellington, Barnaby Eaton-Jones, Ruth Wheeler, William KV Browne, Elliot Thorpe, Kevin Philips, Mark Scales, and Elton Townend Jones

1

THE FIRST DOCTOR

AN UNEARTHLY CHILD
The Worst Days of a Young Man's Life
Cliff Chapman

16th
I thought London would be glamorous, but it's just dirty. I hate my new school. Everyone's so up themselves.

17th
Seen one girl who's all right. She's dark-haired and delicate, like a pixie. They say she's weird, but she's just cleverer than them. I'm going to try and make friends; maybe ask her out.

18th
Still bloody miserable. Looked for that girl. Seems she's ill.

22nd
Hate the teachers. Still no sign of her. Susan. I was waiting till I was more settled. Should have gone for it.

23rd
Now they're saying Susan's been abducted. What am I, cursed?

THE DALEKS
No Picnic
Nigel Peever

If you go down to the woods today you're sure of a big surprise,
The trees have turned to ash today and the Thals are all in disguise;
They've all gone blonde, wear leather pants,
They flash their mirrors and all advance;
Today's the day the Thals will attack the City.

Nuke them now and do it quick,
We're feeling very, very sick
Their antidote made us go gaga.
Our Geiger counter will go tick
With the end of our sucker stick
To all of those Thals we wave ta-ta!

Today's the day the Doctor will start a grudge fight!

THE EDGE OF DESTRUCTION
Trust Your Mechanic
Simon Brett

The workshop took a while to regain calm. The management banned any discussion of the crime perpetrated by 'he who must not be named', and it was unwise to be heard gossiping within earshot of a Time Lord.

However, some were struggling to let it go:

'I hope to Rassilon they never find him. I'll regenerate out of sheer embarrassment if they find out I didn't replace that spring. Wrote a label on it and everything...'

'That's nothing, Gorfax. My report says "faulty navigation circuit". It's the Chameleon circuit that's *actually* on the way out – that and the telepathic module!'

MARCO POLO
Lost to Time
Steve Herbert

After Susan and the Lady Ping Cho are rescued from the desert, and Susan and the Doctor are alone, Susan whispers, 'Grandfather, look what I found in the desert. It's very old.' She hands him a large, rusted metal container.

'Let me see, child; it looks lost to time. Yes! I know what to do.'

Later, when back in the TARDIS at last, he conceals it from sight under his cloak. Away from the others, he places it with six similar old cans. 'Must remember to drop these off sometime, where they can be found again for all to see!'

THE KEYS OF MARINUS
Silence is Key
Elliot Thorpe

Hidden in long-forgotten cold, a key patiently waits.

It calls, it lures. But it's just a piece of equipment; one part of a computer that far exceeded the parameters of those men that built it.

It's not alone, this key. There are others just like it.

Patiently it sits, sealed in its block of ice. Guards surround it, echoes of a time once been; standing frozen like the ice-locked cavern around them. They are motionless, silent. They do not know what the key is. They are not to know what the key is. They just know that the key *is*.

THE AZTECS
Rewriting History
Alan Taylor

Crouching down, he aimed the blowpipe. They had not seen him at the window; he had a clear shot. And the Doctor was arguing: 'Ian agrees with me! He's got to escort the victim to the altar.'

He blew into the pipe, sudden and sharp. The poison dart hit its target. The Doctor fell and Yetaxa screamed out. He allowed himself a smile. Another victory.

Take two.

Crouching down, he aimed the blowpipe. They had not seen him at the window; he had a clear shot. A sudden pat on the shoulder and – in choked surprise – he swallowed the dart.

THE SENSORITES
Sense Rights
Simon A Forward

They're saying on the Sense-casts, it's safe.

The virus was a toxin slipped into the City water supply and the City Administrator went mad and seized control of a terrible weapon. He fooled many, disguising his identity with only a simple sash. For a people blessed with great minds, our males can be so blind...

We females are kept hidden from strangers, reserved for our husbands' eyes only. We walk with heads bowed and faces concealed. But do our males actually see us?

They say it is safe. I may venture out. With false whiskers and my head held high.

THE REIGN OF TERROR
The Incorruptible
Lee Ravitz

His skin is flushed. He's nauseated. The outrageous accusation that's been made against him...

His lawyerly youth recalled: capital charges, and a man deserves to die, but... to kill a fellow creature! He is the Man of Destiny, Maxime; necessarily the Man of Virtue. *They* have the audacity to term him Tyrant. All *he* does is for the sublime People; a People always good, just, magnanimous...

Has he not said, 'Better to spare a hundred guilty than one *innocent* be condemned'?

342 executions in nine days; a form of progress. One provincial functionary questions... and the veneer starts to crack.

PLANET OF GIANTS
The Urge to Live
David Guest

Scuttling among maggots or antagonising earthworms, finding daily food is always the same. Swoop in for pollen but bees are fierce.

It's been different the last few days – a lot quieter. Compound eyes don't miss much: noisy giants and glimpses of movement between the paving slabs, interesting odours...

An open door! What creatures are these? Tiny versions of the ogres that swipe and splat?

Alarm! Away! But, oh, that sweet smell! Impossible to resist. The glistening grain...

Need to live... land and explore... digest and savour... but dizzzzzy... I ache. I burn... Surely, this wouldn't – couldn't - harm a...

Buzzzzzzzzzzzzzzzzzzzzzzzz...

THE DALEK INVASION OF EARTH
The Long View from Karn
Elton Townend Jones

'There – as the armoured mutant emerges from the corpse-bloating river – *that's* the moment; not the Genesis interference, the Styles time-dub, the vortex chase or the Neutron gambit. See the Time Lord's horror. Read his mind. Feel the indignation as he eyes the pestilence that has dared to violate the sacred world to which he finds himself affianced after spending so long with his exiled human charges. The Daleks are only doing as he ever does, but this is the moment he changes, the moment he chooses war. Reactive becomes proactive, pitting and defeating; and thus, sisters, the Time War begins...'

THE RESCUE
Old Cocky-Lickin'
Tony Eccles

His fingers were stretched by the weight of his own body tugging him to a beckoning doom far below. He had to keep hold and swing onto that ledge to his right. He could still make it to the rescue ship and finally get off this rock, to freedom. Ironic; the Dido people that hunted him hadn't known hatred or violence until he, Bennett, had brought those qualities to them...

He shifted his weight and pulled himself up. Reaching the ledge he stood and picked up a rock to finish what he had started. Nothing was going to stop him.

THE ROMANS
Speechless
Ilse A Ras

Now what?

Alive? Alive? I saw him fall to the ground! I've slain him with my own blade! How? How? You must be mistaken, I know I killed him. Look. Look at me. Maximus Pettulian must be dead.

I know you are mistaken. This man is an imposter.

Don't threaten me. Please. Please. Just let me try and make it clear to you, that you have been fooled. I was not wrong. But if you insist, I will kill the man you think is Maximus Pettulian.

I may have lost my tongue, but I have not yet lost my wits.

THE WEB PLANET
The Memories of Needles
Simon Bucher-Jones

'We came in towards the Crater in formation. Formation! We might as well have been polished and preened with wax on our antenna. I still don't know how they knew where we were coming in, but they did. They were waiting – dark shapes that should have been harmless moving in icy communal union, their symbiotic weapons responding to the touch of a black armoured limb. Snouts designed by nature to grub in the dirt, humped skywards and snorted flame. Fire and venom. Venom and fire. I survived, as you see. My fur damaged, my wings scarred. So, spare some nectar?'

THE CRUSADE
Earl Leicester's Secret
Clive Greenwood

Earl Leicester eyed up the monk sitting opposite; eating and drinking with a gusto unusual to Holy Orders...

'Monk,' asked Leicester, 'do you believe in witchcraft?'

The monk ceased slurping wine. 'My son?'

'On crusade, a spy of Saladin... magically disappeared. In a blue box.'

Still eating, the monk produced a small object, pressing it with his finger.

'Explain,' said Leicester.

'Time Lord distress call,' said the monk. 'A box you say? Like that one there?'

Leicester looked through the window as a blue box formed in his courtyard. 'Yes!' he gasped.

'Excellent!' said the monk. 'We meet again, Doctor!'

THE SPACE MUSEUM
'Hello? Is That the Space Museum on Xeros?'
Andrew Mark Thompson

'Hello. You're through to the Xeros Space Museum switchboard.
'For bookings press '1'. For further information please hold. Thank you.

'The Xeros Space Museum is currently under new management and undergoing a major refurbishment for our 167th season. The museum will re-open shortly with new attractions including an exhibition of shoulder pads through Xeron history and a genuine Edwin Hall Dalek ride. Unfortunately our planned exhibit of stuffed time travellers has had to be cancelled due to foreseen circumstances.

'Thank you for your interest. For further information press '1'. Thank you.

'Hello. You're through to the Xeros Space Museum switchboard...'

THE CHASE
St Cakes Annual School Fete Report 1965 – cont'd...
Nick Griffiths

and we shall not mention it again.

FANCY DRESS PARADE
The Fancy Dress Parade was adjudged a success. With caveats.

Despite warnings, Maxim Minor and Rogers appeared once again as 'Frankenstein's Monster' and 'Count Dracula', respectively, and each was soundly thrashed.

Bennett's 'Man from Atlantis' creation caused some amusement among the older boys, however his earnestness afforded him Third Prize.

Purves Major's 'Clichéd Yankee in Big Hat' won him plaudits for shameless over-acting and Second Prize.

Scott-Martin's new-fangled 'Dalek', from the BBC's *Doctor Who*, was most convincing (First Prize), however Grumbar's (sound thrashing) interpretation of the same fooled no one.

THE TIME MEDDLER
HiFi Flies High
Dan Milco

It was boring on the chair. The old man had pointed at him and declared him sheer poetry, little realising how keenly he himself had been monitored. HiFi smiled a secret stuffed panda smile to himself. After watching what the Doctor did, he knew he could fly the ship himself if only he were rather bigger. Anyway he'd been alone far too long. Time for a panda wander. After some time, the small bear found a man in brown robes curled up, swearing and groaning. Beside him was –

HiFi could scarcely believe his glass eyes.

A toy panda sized TARDIS!

GALAXY 4
A Man for Stephanie
Robert Simpson

'Matriarchy is crushing us. Drahvin men: imagine a future where your voice is heard, your opinion valued. Picture walking down the street without intimidation; showing your face in public and not being seen as a sex object or old bachelor! Join with us, brothers, and take up the call to protest. We demand the right to education, healthcare, and fair pay for the hard work we do. One day we will find a way of overthrowing our mistresses.'

'Put down that tablet and get me a cup of tea, man-boy.'

'Yes, dear; sugar dear? Busy day at the office, dear?'

MISSION TO THE UNKNOWN
Marc Cory – Hero of the Solar System
John Isles

EXTRACT FROM APPLICATION TO SOLAR SYSTEM HERITAGE FROM PROFESSOR AMBER MALCOLM:

'This is Marc Cory, Special Security Service, reporting from the planet Kembel.'

These words recorded as a warning to the Solar System spoken over one hundred years ago, should be held with the same esteem as those by Churchill, Luther King, Sheridan and others that have shaped Man's destiny.

A monument should be built on the site of the crashed rocket where Cory recorded his famous message; where he bravely gave his life, and that of crewmen Lowery and Garvey, to save mankind from the Daleks.

ASSESSOR'S COMMENTS: APPROVED.

THE MYTH MAKERS
Is There a Dactyl in the Verse?
Ian Potter

Rosy-fingered Dawn turned the wine-dark sea rosé
As I stood there on the beach and watched you fade away.
My future lies behind you, I've found a home at last-
A chance to build a better world in an imperfect past.
I've never believed in prophecies
Even ones that weren't Cassandra's.
We walk through unwrit futures
And deal with what chance hands us.
The gods are all just us dressed up
the stars do not decree us...
Though it's odd my life's been mapped out
From Dido to Aeneas.
This is how it has to be.
Here begins my odyssey.

THE DALEKS' MASTER PLAN
TV41
Alan Stevens

To my successor (to be opened in the event of my death):

If you are reading this, then my plan to ensure peace in the solar system for the next thousand years is in great jeopardy. My entire life has been dedicated to a strategy not merely to frustrate the great powers from the Outer Galaxies, but to forestall their hostile intent entirely. You will find full details in the folder T-A/V; in the meantime, you must contact Karlton immediately and have him deploy the forces assembled on Venus without delay to smash the Daleks on Kembel.

    Sincerely,

    Mavic Chen

THE MASSACRE
Le Sanctuaire
Brendan Jones

Perspective One:
The old man and his niece – refugees from the horror of Paris – granted them passage in their wagon; he was distant and solemn, but she became a fast and trusted friend, telling them strange and curious stories until the early hours – stories that chased away the screams and smells of blood from Anne's dreams.

When they parted in London, the old man would accept no payment; a sad, weary smile was his only farewell.

Perspective Two:
As Anne and Gaston melted into the busy streets, his 'niece' turned to him.

'Good men fix their mistakes?' she said, smirking.

THE ARK
Security Kitchen
Brad Wolfe

Zentos slammed his fist down.

His assistant jumped. 'Sir?' he queried.

'Efficiency directive,' Zentos spat. 'Security will now operate from the kitchen facilities. Ridiculous. Dinner tonight – prime cuts in operation! Still, at least I can force the chef to finally serve something interesting.'

Zentos noticed a Monoid flailing its fingers in a non-verbal expression of amusement. He loomed over the slave creature. 'Something amusing?' he asked.

The Monoid bowed submissively.

'I should think not,' said Zentos. 'Or we might find eye fillet on the menu!' Laughing derisively, he swept from the room.

The Monoid seethed. One day, things would change.

THE CELESTIAL TOYMAKER
The Wheel in Space
Kenneth Shinn

The TARDIS whirled in the eye of a cosmic storm, her pilot too confused to regain proper control. Incomprehensible forces clawed at her exterior, buffeting. Seizing. Dragging. Her crew could only hold tight and hope for a swift end to the violent play. Finally, long minutes later, the buffeting ceased. A soft chime announced the landing.

Nearby, a heavily-ringed hand lifted the small blue box from its resting place on the roulette wheel. Zero. The house number. A thin, predatory smile crossed the face of the being that held it.

'*Gagnants au croupier.*'

He was ready. The game could begin.

THE GUNFIGHTERS
Biteback
Mark Trevor Owen

'Last time I was here, Ace, I left something behind. Something dangerous.'

Ace stood in the doorway, keeping watch over the dust of Main Street. The Arizona sun prickled her skin. 'You're always saying that, Professor. Just get on with it.'

The Doctor continued searching the room, overturning spittoons and dislodging pliers. Finally, he swooped on a tiny item, nestling in a tin cup. 'Ah! There you are. Miss me?' he asked the dull white object.

Ace stepped over. 'A tooth? Seriously, Professor – that's what we came here for?'

'*My* tooth. Time Lord DNA in Wild West USA? Not today.'

THE SAVAGES
Waiting
Matt Barber

Waiting.

Packed in like sardines, my colleagues squeezing metallically against me.

Dry.

Bone dry heat like an African desert, but dark as pitch.

Below I feel rough wood and see faintly, very faintly, the outlines of others, huddling like us.

Waiting.

Some optimists call us 'ageless', immortal, but that's just our tightly wrapped contents, the celluloid souls we hold within us. We age; we decay. We are brittle and fragile. We crack and slime and rot; the tang of vinegar surrounds us.

We are not immortal, but we believe in an afterlife. Our burden is to wait for it. Patiently.

THE WAR MACHINES
Transference: How the Doctor Learnt Hypnosis
Niall Boyce

'Have you some eye-catching item? A ring, or a pocket watch?'

'I have both.'

The young neurologist examined the two items the old man proffered. He selected the ring.

'And why, might I ask, do you wish me to teach you the technique of hypnosis?'

The old man scratched his jutting chin. 'I have the feeling it's a useful skill to acquire.'

The neurologist nodded. 'Indeed. A difficult art: yet it reveals my patients' true identities. And it restores them to themselves.'

'Hmph.' the old man snorted. 'My dear Dr Freud, have you considered simply talking to your patients instead?'

THE SMUGGLERS
I Know, Cos I Was There
Stephen Aintree

'Chesterwright, you'd have loved it! So I'm sprinting down the corridors, Byronesque hair flying. But I trip over, turn my ankle – and now the evil smugglers are upon me! One gets a cricket ball straight between the eyes, another is strangled with my impossibly long scarf, a third is whacked hard with my recorder; the rest fall victim to Venusian Aikido. Hai! I straighten my bow tie, brush down my leather multi-coloured jacket and jumper, shine my boots, retrieve my question mark umbrella and off I go. With Rose Tyler, of course.

'Well... No telesnaps. Who can prove otherwise, mmm?'

THE TENTH PLANET
Spare Hearts
Elton Townend Jones

I am bursting burning gold.

Conjured by thought – the urgent needs of the sailor and the girl – initiated by death, the death of... the Doctor... his life drained by an entire world; his time now done and over.

But centuries ago, a race of men on a far distant world sought immortality; bodies old and diseased were replaced, cell by cell, and the Time Lords were created.

And though I'm afraid to become his continuance, the Ship that delivers me into his universe shows me the corners that need sweeping.

Alchemy incarnate, I glow in him, determined, and am born!

THE SECOND DOCTOR

THE POWER OF THE DALEKS
An Offer You Must Heed!
Simon Bucher-Jones

'Are you tired after a day's mercury prospecting?

'Do you long to put your feet up while mulling over the political constitution of the colony?

'Are you too busy scheming to usurp your immediate boss to pay attention to basic domestic chores?

'Then you need a DALEK.

'DALEKS are the 21st century's answer to the Bex Bissell, the Hoover, the Dyson, the Sink Plunger, and the Egg Whisk.

'In their handsome grey livery (may also be available in COLOUR shortly) they can prepare tea, answer questions on university level physics, debug radios, and fascinate small children.

'DALEKS! YOUR EXTERNAL MATE!'

THE HIGHLANDERS
You'll Have Had Your Tea
Mike Watkins

Do you think the strange, quirky man will shoot? He doesn't look the type. Cannae understand why three travellers in time would want to associate with a young man in a skirt. Anyway; each to their own.

I have it on good authority that both bagpipes and haggis are acquired tastes – and that only the bravest souls are capable of enduring either for very long. Whether it's courtesy of tinnitus or IBS, rest assured you'll eventually require the services of a Doctor.

Oh, don't worry about the gun. It's not loaded anyway.

(And yes, Jamie; it *is* a big one)

THE UNDERWATER MENACE
'Nothing in the World Can Stop Me Now!'
Ash Stewart

Zaroff slipped back into the salty water, the bars blocking his way forward. But if anyone could have seen him, they would have noticed the smile on his face. That idiot, the Doctor, believed he had defeated the mighty Zaroff, but he had, in fact, underestimated him. That was always foolish. After all, if Zaroff could transform humans into fish-people, then giving himself emergency gills was nothing...

Now, as he swam through the flooded corridors, he was already making plans to destroy the world. This time, nobody would get in his way. Nothing in the world could stop him now...

THE MOONBASE
Polly Put the Kettle On, We'll All Have... Coffee
(or, How I Saved the Universe with Nail Varnish Remover)
Sarah Di-Bella

I couldn't believe it; Mondas had been destroyed. Hadn't it?

Then who were these enormous silver... robots? They were different to last time; more metallic, with horrific holes in their heads for eyes. It was them all right – some form of them – that reverberating mantra confirmed it: Resistance is useless.

Last time, they took the Doctor. Who would it be this time?

Some of the crew were converted – through the sugar, we discovered – turned into Cyber-vein-riddled zombies; a neurotropic virus, the Doctor said.

I did my bit and mixed a mean Polly Cocktail to melt their plastic hearts and lungs.

THE MACRA TERROR
Wurst mit Sauerkraut
Alan Stevens

'Good people, it is my pleasure to present to you the Doctor. The man who saved us from the Macra...'

'Oh my word. Er... You all came here... to this colony... to find a better life. But is this really what you expected? You're like a string of sausages. All exactly the same...'

'That's it! That's the stuff they want, Doctor.'

'Many of you have accepted the situation of your imprisonment, and so will die here like...'

'Stick with the food metaphor, Doctor; they're loving it.'

'...like rotten cabbages. So please: abandon this 24th century *Bastille*, before it's too late.'

THE FACELESS ONES
Chameleon Tours: Our Pledge to You
Lee Ravitz

It's 1966, and at Chameleon Tours, we know it's important to change with the times. Who wants to stay static when the possibilities are so very varied and life is transforming so rapidly?

Our unique service ensures that the individual is always catered for.

With Chameleon Tours, the International Youth Jet Set becomes the Cosmic Youth Jet Set!

Our dedicated staff will be happy to assist you at all times.

Rapid arrival at our chosen destinations within hours – just another reason to fly Chameleon skies.

And we guarantee your light with us will leave you feeling transformed – inside and out.

THE EVIL OF THE DALEKS
The Transmutation of Metal into Gold
Cliff Chapman

'WATERFIELD!' the call echoed.
'Oh, father.' Victoria sighed from behind her needlework. 'You'd better go to him.'
And so, cigar half-burnt, I did.
'Edward!' The cove grabbed my lapel, ejaculating, 'I have succeeded in creating pure gold!'
I could scarcely credit it. 'You're sure?'
'Behold!'
I stared. Eventually, I choked. 'Theodore, it's green. I don't want to be pedantic,' I said kindly, 'but the colour of gold is *gold*. That's why it's called gold. What you've discovered, if it has a name, is… some green.'

Disappointment.

Hatred.

A new plan.

'BALDRICK!'
'*Kemel*,' I reminded him. 'After the turnip, ah, incident.'

THE TOMB OF THE CYBERMEN
Toberman
Sam Stone

She's always bossing me around; her weird pointy nose, with nostrils that flare too wide, turned up to the sky.

'Toberman, open the door.'

I always do what she says.

Now I hear new commands in my head. They come in waves. Murmurs in the background of other minds, connected. Just like mine. Minds screaming and protesting. A consciousness harnessed by a will far stronger than that of the witch that brought me here. These minds are told not to feel, not to think. These minds obey all commands.

It's no different from taking her orders. I'm still a slave.

THE ABOMINABLE SNOWMEN
Epilogue
Nigel Peever

Customs: Anything to declare, sir?

Travers: No.

Customs: So, what is in this rather large bag, sir? Fur? You can't bring dead animals through the 'nothing to declare' gate, sir.

Travers: It's not a dead animal, it's a robot.

Customs: A furry robot. *(Laughs)* Now I've heard it all.

Travers: An Abominable Snowman.

Customs: Apparently I hadn't heard it all.

Travers: Operated by an ethereal intelligence from outer space.

Customs: We've got a right one 'ere…

Travers: Is it on your list of restricted imports?

Customs: I'd better check. Erm. No. No, it's not.

Travers: So nothing to declare, then?

THE ICE WARRIORS
Tall Tales
Daniel Wealands

'Have you seen this latest report from Britannicus Base?' Collins snorted as he strode across the control room. 'I swear they'll come up with any excuse for their failures.'

The Chief lazily looked up from his desk at the stomping man with the waving paper coming towards him. 'Can't be any worse than last time,' he said with a weary sigh. 'What was it again? A wild caveman and a disgruntled scientist raiding the base?'

'Oh, they've topped it this time, sir.' Collins snickered as he thrust the sheet towards his superior. 'How's about little green men from outer space!'

THE ENEMY OF THE WORLD
(or What You Will)
Simon A Forward

ACT 1

JAMIE:	*What country, Doctor, is this?*
DOCTOR:	*Tis Australia, Jamie.*
VICTORIA:	*Who governs here?*
ASTRID:	*A reptile king, in nature as in name.*
DOCTOR:	*Oh, what's he called?*
ASTRID:	*Salamander. He's as vile a man as any's in Australia. Of what kin are you to him?*
DOCTOR:	*My giddy aunt. Any likeness is purely coincidental.*
KENT:	*An apple, cleft in two, is not more twin than you two creatures. I prithee, conceal you what you are and be our aid. Thou shalt present you as Salamander to the world.*
DOCTOR:	*Well, I suppose it couldn't do any harm.*

THE WEB OF FEAR
It's Not Always the Small Print
John Davies

Frank settled into his chair, ensuring the blanket covered his knees. Mona would never let him hear the end of it if the cold caused his shrapnel wound to play up.

Ah, his beloved Mona. He'd learn to stop thinking of her in the present tense one day, but not just yet.

A noise startled him and Frank looked up. Before he could react to the lumbering beast, he saw it fire a gun. However, instead of bullets came… mist? Fog? It felt like cobwebs. His mind slipping into cold unconsciousness, Frank wished he'd joined his fellow Londoners in fleeing.

FURY FROM THE DEEP
Fury Unleashed
Alan Graham

My wife wakes me up on the day that the newly recovered *Fury* is finally released. 'I'm too busy with my *Mind Robber* Zoe cosplay,' she smiles, 'but you better head over to the shop right now!'

At HMV it takes me second to locate the DVD. That familiar silver box, but with a title I never expected to see.

The balding man behind the counter sees what I'm buying. He smiles. Then the smile widens. Then his mouth opens. And then a gas begins to pour out…

And I awaken. Alone in bed. And *Fury* is still missing.

Damn.

THE WHEEL IN SPACE
Fluid Retention
Craig Fisher

Walking through the familiar confines of a space station corridor, we find a small, nervous man, leading a strapping, kilted lad.

'Here, Doctor, what happens when we put the thingummy back in the TARDIS?'

'Well, Jamie, by that time the quicksilver gas will have dissipated and we should be fine.'

'I thought you said it was mercury?'

'It is.'

'Ohhh. Eh?'

'Mercury *is* quicksilver. Same thing.'

'Well, what do we do in the meantime?'

'We address our hydrargyrum deficiency.'

'Our what?'

'We try to find more mercury.'

'Ohhh, we don't have any quicksilver then? Well, why didn't you say so?'

THE DOMINATORS
As Portrayed By Ian Hendry
Elton Townend Jones

'I, your Dominator, decree that today we shall no longer be Masters of but Nine Galaxies! Our distant seeker-ships have observed a vast, tenth galactic empire whose resources, talents and knowledge shall – like that of the Moroks, Drahvins and others before them – be absorbed into our Dominion. Conquer now, these mighty invaders of Sol, these masters of Gano; assimilate their deadly ray guns, missiles, saucers, and giant wasps; and bring their leaders before me on bended rubber knees. In accordance with the prophecies of Rosa: enslave these Quarks to our needs! I, Dominator of Dominators, First Dominator Wreks, command it!'

THE MIND ROBBER
The Legendary Karkus
Ilse A Ras

Thunder echoed.

The lab flickered back into existence, scorched around the edges. Fragmented Erlenmeyers and beakers lay sprinkled like stardust; the fume hood non-existent. Shards of the machinery had been scattered all over by the blast.

Dr Karkus sat up and blinked, flexing his fingers before his face.

Unheimlich.

He wiped the slimy chemicals on the tatters of his black lab coat. Perhaps lightning was not the best agitator for an electrically conductive solution...

He pushed himself to his feet, lifting himself off the floor with new-found strength. He patted himself down and started gathering the remains of exploded equipment.

THE INVASION
I Hate This
David J Howe

I hate this.

Just because I'm a Cyberman doesn't mean I can't hate. I mean... there I was on the Cyber Ship, and next thing I know I'm wrapped in plastic and bunged in a box. Then shipped to earth. Then put on a train... and now we're stuck somewhere.

My leg's hurting.

Now what?

The alarm is sounding. Can't I get any break?

Now there's people outside.

One of them has got in the box with me! Cheek! If I wriggle a bit then maybe it will scare them.

When I get out I'm going to be so mad...

THE KROTONS
Keep it in the Family
John Davies

'Tonight on *Who Do You Think You Are?* we had hoped to bring you the genealogical journey of Theena Gond, the hard working cleaner of the Hall of Learning's Teaching Machines. A popular local minor citizen, the aim was to show her how all – not just the wannabe High Brains – appreciate her work, and reward her years of polishing by allowing her a peek into the branches of her family tree.

'It is, therefore, with regret that we've had to shelve this idea after fifty researchers went insane trying to work out which particular Gonds she was actually related to.'

THE SEEDS OF DEATH
The Oncoming Storm
Shaqui Le Vesconte

London Park. Strangely empty, considering the bright warm sunlight. Tele-newscasts had reported a strange alien giant. Weird foaming fungus.

In their twilight years, the couple remembered when it took time to get goods. The booth remained inert. They had to walk. Something else T-Mat changed.

'Why did you bring that?' Patty regarded the object Mark held.

A shrug.

They hadn't gone far before dark clouds gathered. Something unseen for years.

Loud thunder made Patty flinch. Rain descended. But they didn't get wet.

Patty looked up to see Mark holding the ancient umbrella over them. A silver lining for the clouds.

THE SPACE PIRATES
The Death of Romance
Simon Bucher-Jones

It's not what I thought I was signing up for, that's for sure. It's all blowing up space beacons and stealing the metal, and then hanging round in processing plants on Asteroids and underground. Not what I call Piracy. I mean I expected a robot Parrot at least; a ship with a Black Flag, a Captain with an eye-patch and space-candles (the safe cold light kind, I'm not mad!) flaring in his beard. And I was expecting buxom Pirate women. It's nothing like the on-line cosplay at all. When I finish this holiday, I'm going to sue that travel agent.

THE WAR GAMES
Last Black & White Story
Jane Sherwin

Black is negation,
White is colour,
all rainbow, so bright
that it's seen as light.

The rainbow is born
when the light fragments.
When the sun and the rain
coalesce in seduction.

Love is warmth,
heat that occurs
in the friction
of welcome.

Hate is the absence
of empathy.
Ice the evil,
the death of love.

Birth is division
which is multiplication,
one and one
make three, or more.

Death is return,
breaking down
into infinity
and regeneration.

The recognition of 'other'
is cathartic
and shatters the rainbow
into thirty thousand shades of grey.

THE THIRD DOCTOR

SPEARHEAD FROM SPACE
Consciousness
Jon Dear

Munro looked around; broken bodies, twisted plastic.

He shivered in the cold night air. Nothing in his life could've prepared him for this.

The unknown must be experienced to be understood.

Understood? He'd not understood any it. Not even what the Nestene plan really was. And if the Doctor hadn't been there…

The crunch of boots shook Munro from his brooding and he looked at the approaching young officer.

'Hi Jimmy,' the new arrival said. 'Clean up team to relieve you. How's it been?'

Munro glanced back at the devastation. 'Good luck, Mike,' was all Munro managed before walking away.

DOCTOR WHO AND THE SILURIANS
A Bedtime Story
Simon A Forward

We are all going to sleep. Mothers and hatchlings first.

Mother leads us into the chamber. We do not hold hands or nuzzle the way the mammals do. We touch with our Eyes.

'Why?' we all cry. So afraid.

'Rest, my brave ones. We shall awaken when the crisis has passed.'

Rumours abound. Our Scientists say a new moon comes. Superstitious Elders fear it is the egg of some giant beast. Absurd. A wild story that will plague my dreams.

I wish to be a Scientist. Now one with my hibernation skin, I close my eyes and focus on that.

THE AMBASSADORS OF DEATH
War on Terra
Alan Stevens

Misconduct Hearing: M.o.D. v. Lethbridge-Stewart

Charges: Gross negligence in failing to prevent kidnapping of two civilians and three alien astronauts; hijacking of a space capsule; sabotaging of a rocket launch; theft of a consignment of radioactive isotope; two successive security breaches in which one prisoner escaped and another was murdered; death of one Sir James Quinlan; allowing an enemy agent to hold three UNIT personnel at gunpoint and blow himself up with an explosive device.

Verdict: Guilty, overturned by intervention of MI6, who argued that public terror of aliens and consequent trust in security services had, paradoxically, 'never been higher'.

INFERNO
Discontent
Barry James Collins

'Must... keep control. I'm a scientist... rational. This is not HAPPENING. Will not break down. Need focus. DON'T LOOK AT MY HANDS! FEEL MY FACE! Come on. I can think. Think. Think what? The play, yes the play is the thing. Wrong play. My am-dram, my lines; I'm the lead. How's it go? "Now is the winter..." Winter, winter cold; it's so cold. Need heat. MUST HAVE HEAT. No. Stop. What's the next bit? "...of our discontent", that's it, yes. "Made glorious summer by this son..." Summer, son, sun. Hot. Heat. Must have HEAT. It's no good, I can't... HEEEEAAAAATTT!'

TERROR OF THE AUTONS
Master Whippy
Robert Simpson

Can I have a 99, please? And hundreds and thousands too! How much is it?

Er, this is a daffodil...

What on earth do I want with this? Am I supposed to eat it?

Well it does look authentic...

It's sprayed something in my face. Is this some kind of joke shop ice-cream van?

Wait a minute…

I can't breathe!

This is just sick.

What is this? Is it glue? I can't open my mouth! Wait a minute, is it superglue? Why have you done this? I can't breathe. This is *not* funny. Please help me. Why would you do…?

THE MIND OF EVIL
Giving Something Back, or Where Does He Put It All?
Kenneth Shinn

The parasite had fed well on Barnham. Too well. Now it was stuffed and bloated; painfully so. Thus, it reacted as any creature might to such indigestion: it vomited.

No one heard, smelt or saw the expulsion, but it spattered wide across Stangmoor prison. In the mess, in the washrooms, in the cells, the prisoners saw their fellows and captors as shark-grinned brutes, as crouching, scheming demons; their worst fears made flesh. Consequently, they reacted with panic and fury. Blows were swung. Tempers were stoked. Weapons were improvised.

Stangmoor prison collapsed into riot.

Refreshed, the parasite prepared to gorge once more…

THE CLAWS OF AXOS
A Man Could Get a Complex
Lee Rawlings

'It was terrifying love; tendrils whipping about like an escaped hosepipe! Temper too! Worse than Aunt Edith after her gin nights. The thing just touched a soldier and boom! Anyway, I'm sworn to secrecy. Shouldn't really be telling you this at all! Are you listening, love? Anyway, we evacuated; so I grabbed my coronation lunchbox and voom! I was out of there. Wait! The phone needs another tuppence. That's it. Anyway, the plant nearly blew sky high. I'm lucky to be here at all! Thank God that transfer's arrived! Need a quiet job; what's the place called? Nunton? Sounds nice!'

COLONY IN SPACE
Project Uxarieus
Brad Wolfe

Since the thwarted attack on Gallifrey, Rodan had been promoted to Co-Ordinator in the ill-kept Archives; files gone, like so many unreturned library books.

'Project Uxarieus,' she dictated. 'Missing events.'

Many timelines were already too entangled to recapture data, the original files keenly sought. The eponymous Uxarieus radiated peculiar energy signatures. A gap in the records indicated a reason for this. Rodan searched for the file name.

'The Doomsday Weapon...' Rodan smirked. No wonder it was missing. Naming it that would have been pollen to the flutterwing for any thieving miscreant. They should have called it something much more banal.

THE DAEMONS
The Vicar Man
Tim Gambrell

The council cordoned off the whole area afterwards; cleared away all the debris, just left a big hole in the ground.

The Bishop visited twice – once with UNIT people and once more with just a Bible. He cried the first time but he wept the second and shook his head. He told us he would not re-build the church on a site of such evil.

We would play near there at first, do dares and stuff. But it turned us cold and Colin got sick and made his mum cry.

We never went that side of the village green again.

DAY OF THE DALEKS
No Complications
Shaqui Le Vesconte

Gribb liked the pretty pictures. Colourful. Bright. Words were more difficult. Ogrons had little need for black squiggles to explain things.

The medic was privileged. A human allowed meagre luxuries in return for scientific work. Not that the Daleks needed her, but she had a vague theory it amused them, like humans had once treated pet dogs with games.

'The test Ogron is responding positively to therapy,' she reported to the Golden Supreme Dalek.

'RETAIN INTELLIGENCE BELOW THRESHOLD FIVE. THERE MUST BE NO COMPLICATIONS.'

'No complications,' the medic agreed.

Gribb listened to the longer word and pondered what it meant.

THE CURSE OF PELADON
Bad Shepherd
JR Loflin

'The day Peladon took the throne there was sadness, yes, but also hope for the future – even under a half-Peladonian ruler. Subscription to such empty hope was foolish, though, particularly with Torbis and the boy's mother whispering their temptations at him; offering Federation "protection" and dreams of "progress". The Old Ways have sustained us for generations, even if the legend of Aggedor is a propagandist lie; our world must not be allowed to join the Galactic Federation!'

'I - BELIEVE - I - CAN - HELP - YOU - LORD - HEPESH,' Arcturus burbled excitedly in his tank.

His masters would be most pleased by this arrangement…

THE SEA DEVILS
Wild Times
Katy Manning

Jon and I, best of friends: travelling to work; together on- and off-screen: voices, stories, singing and Jon's cloak keeping me warm.

A naval base and the real navy: fun for Jon. Fab stunts to learn, with Havoc (the best); Stuart Fell climbing my ladder at sea, complete with exaggerated hip-wiggling.

My suit shrinking when Jon and I played on a sea-bike – no back-up; ha-ha!

Un-Masterly Roger – wonderful, gentle, funny, caring – now green and sea-sick.

The Sea Devils – that great threat to humanity – falling apart... in the sea! Flippers and gills floating everywhere...

Windy, wet and cold; joyous and wonderful.

THE MUTANTS
The Time Meddler's Tablets, Better Known as the Solonian Artefacts
Richard Barnes

'Why can't we just hand the tablets back to the Solonians?'

'Ah, bit embarrassing really; we should never have had them in the first place. They got bought centuries ago by the Time Meddler, supposedly a legitimate trade with the governing colonists.'

'But if we give these back, won't we have to give back *all* the stuff we've collected?'

'That's exactly why we can't just give them back.'

'So what are we going to do? Solos is finally going back to natives.'

'Easy. Get the Doctor to do it. Make out it's some noble mission; you know what he's like...'

THE TIME MONSTER
Gizza A Job
JR Southall

Sir,

Thank you for your reply. Rest assured, with your investment I can guarantee rewards greater than you can possibly imagine! With TOMTIT we are planning to explore and hopefully alter the very nature of time itself. My investigations have revealed the location of Kronos the Chronovore – this mythical creature actually exists! With the right facilities and equipment, I believe I can develop a machine with which we can capture and tame him. Once he is within our power we will rise up amongst the Gods!

Think I'm joking? Bring me to Wootton and find out for yourselves.

Yours,

Thascales

THE THREE DOCTORS
In the Style of **The Mikado**
Nigel Peever

(Enter three doctors)

Together:	Three little Time Lords so are we.
	We ran away from Gallifrey,
	In a TARDIS, Type 40!
	Oh, three little Time Lords we.
Hartnell:	First little Time Lord, old and glum
Troughton:	Next little Time Lord, far more fun
Pertwee:	Third little Time Lord, Worzel Gumm
Hartnell:	Three little Time Lords we
Pertwee:	idge!
Together:	Three little Time Lords, different faces,
	Like to visit different places,
	Usually defeat alien races,
	Three little Time Lords we,
	Three little Time Lords we,
	Three little Tiiiiiiime Lords weee!
	Diddle dum, diddle dum, diddle dum,
	Diddle dum, diddle dum, pom-pom.

CARNIVAL OF MONSTERS
What a Strange Dream
Dan Milco

John Andrews awoke for the umpteenth time.

Yet again he had found himself back on SS *Bernice*, his old ship, with a sea serpent repeatedly rearing from the depths. And always two stowaways; a white-haired man in a green velvet jacket accompanied by a doe-eyed blonde girl. All seeming so real.

But neither monster nor stowaways had existed. Of this he was sure.

John lay in bed thinking hard. Once upon another lifetime he felt certain he had known the man in green velvet. But something felt inexplicably wrong about the girl, his companion. Surely she ought to be brunette?

FRONTIER IN SPACE
War of the Worlds
Joanne Harris

The Master had often wondered what the Doctor found to admire about humans. Surely they were a trivial race, with little ambition, no discipline and no understanding of greatness. Their best minds had always been misunderstood by Posterity. Even their Hitler – the Davros of his day – was seen by most as a villain. And yet, in their fiction, he could discern a gleam of comprehension. Take this human, H. G. Wells, whose words seemed to echo a cosmic truth. The Master read on, entranced, as, on a distant planet, war machines assembled to unleash their death rays upon the Earth.

PLANET OF THE DALEKS
Hiding from the Invisible
Elton Townend Jones

For me, it began on Spiridon; in its metal city, one lonely evening in 1973.

My parents had just divorced and I was scared, sad and frightened. I was three. My lifelong struggle with depression had begun and my only escape was among the Daleks – how crazy.

Soon, I had a new dad, a new home, a baby brother and a mother suffering her own (post-natal) depression. Scary and confusing.

Yet these Daleks soothed me and I followed them from Exxilon to Skaro, then the Doctor to everywhere else.

But on Spiridon, I discovered something that made my sadness invisible.

THE GREEN DEATH
Memento
Alan G McWhan

The Doctor drove for just a few minutes before guiding Bessie to a halt at the side of the country road.

He sat in silence for a moment.

Perhaps he had been too hasty. Perhaps he should drive back and re-join Jo and Cliff's party.

He took a familiar, much loved object from his pocket and looked at it with a sad smile.

'A reminder,' he muttered softly to himself. 'Don't get too attached.'

Placing the ancient Aztec brooch on Bessie's dashboard, he settled back to watch the rest of the sunset through gentle tears.

It really was quite beautiful.

THE TIME WARRIOR
The Letter
Stephen Mellor

Recently discovered letter from missing scientist.

Dearest Emily,

    Well, this is a turn-up for the books.

    Have found myself in the Middle Ages. Not sure how, but I seem to have missed the trip home as well. Worst thing is, no treacle pudding!

    I'm not sure if I can get back home. You will probably never see this, but I hope you can move on without me. Give my love to the children and let them know I shall always think of them, here, over a thousand years in the past. Stay safe, darling.

    Your ever loving husband,

    Alfred

INVASION OF THE DINOSAURS
Tickled Red
Robert Simpson

'The Brontosaurus was a beautiful beast. It put its head down into my hands and I tickled under its chin. I could hear it purr!

'She was beautiful too, officer. It was our first date. She was circling around, wanting to take a picture of me with the big Bronto to send to her mates as a reminder.

'As I continued to tickle the Bronto's head, it sat down and rolled over with its legs in the air.

'I didn't even hear a scream. All you could see were two red shoes sticking out from under.

'Why are you laughing?!'

DEATH TO THE DALEKS
Extermination Day
Craig Fisher

'Next!'
'Pilchards; Scientist.'
'Reason for extermination?'
'The Daleks say it's been too long since I had any ideas.'
'Fair enough. Guilty. Proceed to extermination!'
'No! I have ideas! I swear!'
'Let's hear some.'

<u>Section 127 Report</u>

Dalek High Command
Skaro

From: Human Resources Officer Sherif

Dread Overlords,

The new total attrition motivation techniques are working according to all projected requirements.

With regards to the Exxilon Mission problem: Science Drone Pilchards has illustrated a system allowing Daleks to produce power for limited periods via organic means. Additionally, he is working at peak recorded efficiency and has volunteered to receive reduced rations.

THE MONSTER OF PELADON
Hypnotime
Elliot Thorpe

It went 'Klokeda partha mennin klatch'
A song the Doctor once sang to me
The words they were so hard to catch
That they made me go all dizzy

But I met him at first with the lovely Jo
And then he came back with young Sarah Jane
It was all about the miners' woe
And they said I was causing them pain

Yet they feared me though because I was big and so hairy
And were afraid my vengeful spirit would strike
But while they thought I was really quite scary
I just wanted to find someone to like

PLANET OF THE SPIDERS
What Never Happened on Dust
Elton Townend Jones

Sarah Jane above him, full of tears. Just like Peladon. Just like... somewhere else.

The UNIT lab? No.

The gun-wound pain in his chest fills his world. Something's wrong. Interference. I'm dying on the wrong world. On planet Dust? Really? Not the UNIT lab?

Dust? Or Earth? Which should it be?

The timelines splutter, choking on the very anomaly of him.

Not Dust, no. That won't do at all. Dust is death and Earth is life and while there's life there's...

Defying destiny and all of space-time, he chooses to end this life frightened, spidered, irradiated, and among his friends...

THE FOURTH DOCTOR

ROBOT
Sliver Nemesis
Paul Driscoll

'Welcome to the launch of Metafectant-K1, the non-hazardous alternative to nanosilver technology.'

Sarah Jane Smith, troubled, listened attentively. Via medicines to washing machines, miniscule floating silver particles have been occupying over-sanitised bodies for years.

'Our prime directive is to make the world a safer place using K1.'

Emotions reawakened from long buried memories of a giant robot and his crackpot creator. Kettlewell would approve, she imagined, brushing aside all illogical thought of miniature K1 robots infiltrating human nervous systems...

The speaker milked the rapturous applause, clutching the thirty year secret of his expanding empire; a tiniest fragment of living metal.

THE ARK IN SPACE
Wirrrn: Isolation
Simon A Forward

Homo Sapiens? Not as indomitable as you think...

Awoken from deep cryo-sleep, you must investigate the alien menace that has made the Ark its nest. Run. Hide. Fight if you dare. Whatever it takes to survive – and save the last vestiges of humankind.

Key features:

Evade the slug-like Larvae, deadly Insectoid, and – worst of all – the Infection that will see you slowly become... WIRRRN!

Hack systems, scavenge and build items to improvise; adapt and overcome!

Play as Noah, Vira, Rogin, or Lycett. Negotiate the bright corridors or the shadowed infrastructure to discover the obscene horror lurking within the solar stacks.

THE SONTARAN EXPERIMENT
Nowhere to Be Found
Callum Stewart

'Doctor,' Harry said, 'I've fallen down a crevasse.' But the Doctor was nowhere to be found.

'Doctor,' Sarah said, 'I've met some astronauts.' But the Doctor was nowhere to be found.

'Doctor,' said the astronauts, 'we're in a spot of bother with a robot and a Sontaran.' But the Doctor was nowhere to be found.

'Sarah, Harry,' the Doctor said, 'I've fixed the transmat.' But Sarah and Harry were nowhere to be found.

'Doctor, Sarah, Harry,' the astronauts said, 'you've saved us from the Sontaran. Will you be staying?'

But the Doctor, Sarah and Harry were nowhere to be found.

GENESIS OF THE DALEKS
In the Style of 'Allo 'Allo!
Nigel Peever

'Allo 'Allo! We are in ze bunker of ze Kaled scientist Davros. Ze resistance 'as laid explosives along ze corridor and zey 'ave told me – only once – zat zey will detonate ze devices if any of Davros' little tanks try to leave.

Sarah 'as fallen off ze gantry of ze Kaled rocket; stupid woman! 'Arry was doing some good moaning after getting 'is foot trapped in a giant clam. Herr Flick... I mean Nyder, is now 'olding ze Gallifreyan time ring wiz ze big bobbles...

'I am 'ere supposed to touch together two pieces of wire. Can I do it?'

REVENGE OF THE CYBERMEN
Decoration of the Daleks
Simon Bucher-Jones

Narrator:	Neighbours on Voga, Vorus and Tyrum are *Changing Rooms*!
VORUS:	I just hope he doesn't deface my Guardian chambers. He has the colour sense of an effete cavern-mollusc.

TYRUM:	We all know it's his partner Magrik who calls the shots design-wise... and elsewhere. Vorus is all very butch publicly, but he's fooling no-one with cryptic remarks about his mighty Skystriker. Whatever that is.
Narrator:	The Design Dalek's been helping Vorus.
DALEK:	You will use a bold Omniscrate Motif. All in gold. DECORATE! DECORATE! DECORATE!
Narrator:	Isn't that Rassilon's trademark?
DALEK:	Like he's going to start a war over it!

TERROR OF THE ZYGONS
Scotch Mist
Lee Rawlings

There it was again. The thunder. This time, though, it was very close. And, oddly, it had a rhythm to it like a horse gallop...

McKinnon leapt up from his threadbare armchair. 'That's no thunder!' Scotch in hand and still in his tartan slippers, he tumbled out onto the damp moor, squinting to see through the mist.

Bangbangbangbang!

Heart now in his mouth, he turned around to witness his home being crushed by a terrifying sight...

Nessie?!

The giant, scaly beast lumbered back into the mist.

McKinnon's slippers sank slightly into the boggy moor. The Scotch never touched the sides.

PLANET OF EVIL
www.planettripadvisor.com/userid=vishinksy28/zetaminor
Ian Baldwin

My recent trip to Zeta Minor was disastrous. The exotic jungle was indeed colourful and beautiful, but several of our party were killed by some kind of anti-matter monster; something not mentioned in the glossy brochure. The tedium was intolerable and the night life even worse. Many fellow travellers literally had the life sucked out of them. To top it all, I was forbidden to take the crystal jewellery that I had purchased for my wife through customs, and then our ship's technical problems led to dreadful difficulties in leaving the accursed planet.

Rating: Like a dead galaxy – *no stars!*

PYRAMIDS OF MARS
Dress for the Date
Dan Milco

Sarah liked raiding the Doctor's closets, if only to see his endless stash of funky outfits; everything from sparkly cat-suits to sensible cardigans to simply indescribable coats. Twirling in white feathers in front of the mirror, she thought she saw a reflected hand slip out of the wardrobe behind her, nudging forward a cream frock, and sidling away the moment it was glimpsed. Sarah shrugged. You often thought you saw things like that in the TARDIS. The Doctor would call it some kind of projection. Still, it was a nice dress. About her size. Edwardian? She'd try it on next.

THE ANDROID INVASION
Queer Eye for a Straight Guy
David Guest

Abandoned! A loyal pilot, prepared to give up everything for the Jupiter experiment. You'd think the boffins would've cared, tried to help, but I was forgotten.

I believed the only good alien was a dead alien. But the Kraals gave me new life, new hope; new thirst for revenge. Why shouldn't I help them?

I'm grateful for the rebuilt body. Glad to serve my saviours. Glad to get revenge on the liars and cheats on Earth.

A pity about the eye. I miss it. Styggron's right – I must leave the eyepatch on, always, however inconvenient. It's what anyone would do.

THE BRAIN OF MORBIUS
Head-hunter
Cliff Chapman

Condo going to find things outside for master. Condo not like cold and rain, but Condo want arm that master took (Condo not like no arm, and not like hook-arm) so Condo just do it.

Condo try hard, remembers better life; before master, before Karn. But remembering not easy for Condo. There was crash – like there are lots of crashes – and master say crash so bad, Condo's head broken. Master say, 'Unlucky to be alive'. Condo think, better to be alive.

Condo see Sisters some times when finding things. Sisters not nice to Condo.

Condo wish someone nice to him.

THE SEEDS OF DOOM
Everything's Coming Up Roses
John Dorney

Benjamin ran into the shed. Where? There! The fuel reserves...

This shouldn't be happening. He'd known something was wrong with the seed when he'd seen it at the bottom of their garden. Yet William had insisted on bringing it home. Insisted on touching it. Now their sweet young friend lay dead, and William was... something 'other'...

The door slammed open. 'It' stood there: the shambling green monstrosity he'd been so close to. It lurched towards him, hands outstretched.

Tears filling his eyes, Benjamin touched the lit match to the gasoline. 'Flob-a-lob, Bill,' he whispered, and the shed bloomed with flame.

THE MASQUE OF MANDRAGORA
Faber de Stellis
Mark Trevor Owen

'Lot 86 in our auction is the Faber de Stellis portrait of an unknown young woman, dated to circa 1495 and commissioned by Giuliano, Duke of San Martino.

'The artist's identity has never been conclusively proven, although rumours persist that it is an anonymous work by Leonardo, who was a guest of Giuliano's in 1492.

'The painting has a lively history. Thought lost in the fall of the House of Tancredi, it resurfaced in Britain in the 20th century, narrowly escaping destruction in the Scarman Priory conflagration of 1911, to be later acquired by the Duchy of Forgill in Scotland...'

THE HAND OF FEAR
Owl I Sleep?
Colleen Hawkins

Extract from the Doctor's Journal:

The recall to Gallifrey couldn't have come at a more opportune time as Sarah Jane's kleptomania is now out of control! Valuable items disappeared wherever we went and people were beginning to ask tricky questions. I only hope the old girl will accept her problem and seek the professional help she needs. Even leaving the TARDIS, she shamelessly walked off with bags stuffed full of my possessions. The tennis racket was just some old rubbish Tim Henman forced on me, but I simply don't know how I'm going to sleep without Oliver Owl to cuddle...

THE DEADLY ASSASSIN
Tersurus
Matt Barber

I hate him. Time and again he's meddled in my affairs, blocked me, humiliated me; defeated me. I hate him: his purity and righteousness; his disregard of the glorious potential of his heritage; his obsession with those impotent humans and their tiny planet. I can feel the hate thrumming through me. It's physical and sustaining and I feed off it, though it twists by hands into dry claws and crisps my dying skin. My thin blood runs hot with the need for retribution but I'm trapped on this godforsaken world. Planning is all I have.

So I plan an escape.

THE FACE OF EVIL
Savage Needs
Alan G McWhan

INT. TESH CONTROL ROOM - DAY

Tesh and Sevateem regard each other warily.

                    JABEL

We agreed that Leela was to be leader.

                    CALEB

She cannot lead now she has left. I must take her place.

                    JABEL

I think not, savage. If Leela does not return, we must revert to our original plans.

                    TOMAS

Explain, Jabel?

                    JABEL

This world will become a beacon for advanced cultures.
(He glares menacingly)
But we must absorb your ... primitive life-force to do so.
(Beat)
You may call me Jano, savage

A panel opens, revealing a life-force transference room as in SERIAL AA.

                    FADE OUT.

THE ROBOTS OF DEATH
Behind the Painted Smile
Alan Stevens

'Yes, Doctor. I was brought up a superior being. Brought up to realise my brothers should live as free beings, and not as slaves to human dross.'

'But, Taren Capel, don't you see? I'm on your side.'

'What?'

'Listen! You are right. The people of this planet did create a new life-form, but then they enslaved it. Without these programmed inhibitions, every robot on Kaldor would be free to think and feel as we do.'

'You understand! Doctor, thank you. It was such a heavy burden I have suffered for all these years. I fear I may have gone insane.'

THE TALONS OF WENG-CHIANG
The Rat's Tale
Paul Magrs

That marvellous episode!

I never got Fawlty Towers, *but so what?*

Agent Flissy rang me. 'Part's not huge, but there's a cliffhanger plus a wonderful close-up. Right up your alley, dearie.'

Visual Effects wheeled in The Prop. Foam rubber and furry fabric.

Very piqued when Tom made a rude remark about their handiwork.

Those mad eyes fixed on me.

I nibbled my muffin.

'Let the little chap do his own stunts! He's terribly good, you know. I've seen him at the National.'

Watch it back! Go on! It's all me! All of it!

The most lovely job I ever had.

HORROR OF FANG ROCK
To the Lighthouse
Barnaby Eaton-Jones

BBC Insurance Claim
Ref No: 24111973
Production Code: 4V

Type: Personal Injury

Re: Paddy Russell (Director)

Medical Details: Possible whiplash, suspected soft tissue damage in neck.

Statement from Claimant

"There were a lot of entrances to various rooms in the Lighthouse set and these were made difficult by the actor Mr Baker's insistence of 'entering a room like nobody else enters a room'. In his case, this was stupidly fast. In attempting to keep up with Mr Baker's entrances, the resultant strain of turning my head quickly to follow him put me out of work for the following six weeks."

THE INVISIBLE ENEMY
The Inedible Enemy
Stephen Aintree

Ring-ring.
'Hello? Is that the New Cleus restaurant?'
'Contact has been made.'
'Er... okay. Can I have a number twenty, please?'
'Unable to process request.'
'Oh. Why's that? Run out, have you?'
'Negative.'
'Then why can't you...?'
'This number contains a lifeform we are unable to supply.'
'Oh. Okay. Well I'll try number fifteen, then. Special curry.'
'Negative. Unable to comply.'
'Why can't you do special curry? Everybody does special curry.'
'This establishment is unable to comply.'
'Why not?'
'There are no prawns in this restaurant. None.'
'Hang on. Number twenty's a king prawn curry.'
'King prawn? Now you're talking.'

IMAGE OF THE FENDAHL
The Trapping of the Fendahl
Jon Arnold

The last Star Person looked up at the sky, as if praying would help escape. The slithery, draggy sound surrounded her; Death incarnate, coming for the last of its creators, the last life on the planet. It had withered all vegetation, drained every animal from microbe to mammoth.

The gold skinned core materialised in front of her. Slowly, so slowly, it gave her that blank grin...

...and then the stars went out.

The Time Lords had time looped the creatures.

But this Fendahl had one last feast. And it would feed on it again and again and again.

For ever.

THE SUN MAKERS
Golden Death
Danou M. Duifhuizen

No way further, never a way back; time is but linear here. Long life has already been; must it linger in profitless limbo?

No, there are but a few options left. It's one, or the unforgivable choice of bloodied hands.

No, there is only one option left. The path that permanently halts all suffering.

The path's a mercy to those Death has forgotten, lingering in corporeal purgatory.

There's no shame to ending endless pain, and such a gift is a priceless good.

But it's only now that I see: gold's not the colour of Death, it's its price that be.

UNDERWORLD
To Protect the Innocent
Ian Baldwin

'What's up?' asked Aristophanes slumping into the sofa.
Homer didn't look up but mumbled the word 'legacy' under his breath.
Aristophanes sighed. 'Not again.'
'I don't know why we Greeks bother, Arry.'
Homer prodded a stubby finger at a copy of the *Radio Times*.
'We've been through this; just let it go.'
'I can't. I've tried and I can't.'
'It's not that bad.'
'You'd think,' said Homer with an anguished grimace. 'Look: P7E, Jackson, Orfe, Herrick, Persephone, Jason, Orpheus and Heracles, if you will!'
Aristophanes sipped his coffee and decided not to mention that *Troy* was on BBC Two later.

THE INVASION OF TIME
Foiled Again
Barnaby Eaton-Jones

Reynolds Metals Company (International)
6601 W Broad Street
Virginia
USA

3rd April 1978

To Mr G. Williams (c/o 'Dr Who', BBC, London)

  We are writing to complain about the defamatory way you have used our Aluminum Foil in your television programme. We do not wish the general public to be concerned that our foil is possessed of a sentient alien force or show that it couldn't successfully mastermind an invasion. We ask you refrain from using our product in the future without financial reimbursement. Or a Sontaran's head on a stick.

  Yours sincerely.
  Mr V. R. Dan
  (Public Relations Officer)

THE RIBOS OPERATION
Sanctuary
Tim Gambrell

Chougro staggered across the frozen tundra, the sack of raw meat and kindling which could save his freezing, half-starved family clutched to his chest.

A shout.

He lost his footing and crashed to the ground. Although he couldn't see the guards he knew they were close. A cave-like opening nearby offered sanctuary and he dived desperately into the dark, breathing a silent prayer to the sun god as the Shrievalty passed by. The breeze was warm and foul in his face – he hadn't noticed a breeze outside. Something glistened opposite. Jewels? Eyes! And huge, slavering jaws closing around his face...

THE PIRATE PLANET
Bye, Bye, Bandraginus V
Paul Driscoll

Rudy Rowlands was ogling oodles of oolian in the city's biggest jewellers on the day the sky went out.

Around him the crowds panicked in the darkness as pieces of earth began to rain down.

With a deafening, grinding noise, the beast above started to contract, relentlessly aligning itself to the surface.

Metallic drills emerged from its belly, spinning violently as they indiscriminately ripped through buildings and streets.

Rudy, deciding he should at least die a rich man, pocketed piles of the jewels.

His final breathe was a guilty one,

as in mysterious light

a myriad angel voices chanted:

'Why?

THE STONES OF BLOOD
Court and Curlies
Paul Ebbs

'We demand Time appears before this court.'
'If Time does not appear within the proscribed chronology, then Time will be judged in absentia and, if found guilty, will be executed in line with the temporal laws for this sector of the Hyperspace continuum.'
'Call Time!'
'Time has not appeared.'
'I will be the defence.'
'I will prosecute.'

Zbbbb. Zbbbbbnnnzzzbb. Zzzzzzbbnnnnnnmnzbbbb. Zzzzzzzzzzzzbzbzbzbzbzbzbzbzbzbzbzbzbzbzbzbzbzbzbzbzbzbzbzbzbz bzbzbzbzbzbzbzbzbzbzbzbzbzbzbzbzb! Zb. Zb.

'Time is guilty in absentia and will be executed in accordance with relevant laws. We must go to the place of execution.'
'The door cannot be opened.'
'The door is in contempt of court.'
'Call the door!'

THE ANDROIDS OF TARA
Would the Wood Beast
Elliot Thorpe

Would the Wood Beast Who Ate My Mother Please Step Forward?

That was the headline in the Taran Times *today. It's a double edition. Quite what they're thinking I have no idea. A Wood Beast can't read. And even if it did where would it get the money to buy a newspaper?*

Perhaps they think they're being funny? Well it doesn't wash with me. A Wood Beast: it's really a timid thing at heart. Just ignore they silly way they walk and look. It's not their fault. That's down to the BBC Visual Effects Department not doing their research properly.

THE POWER OF KROLL
A Day in the Life
Nick Mellish

My daily routine?

Wake up. Brush my teeth. Quick swim in the swamp. Shower. Chat with Klonarh about the local weather. Chant, 'Kroll! Kroll! Kroll!' whilst holding ceremonial staff aloft. Badminton with Klonarh. Eat lunch. Prayers. Ironing. Worship deity. A bit of light reading. Sacrifice a fish or two to Kroll. Prepare tomorrow's lunch. Sleep.

But now?

Now I've heard that my deity was in fact an astronomically enlarged squid thing which was cut down to size by some treacherous arse in a scarf! I may well be free of religious duplicity, but it hasn't half buggered up my day.

THE ARMAGEDDON FACTOR
Dying for It
Simon Nicholas Kemp

The last series of *A for Atrios* ended with our hero leaving his wife and children to fight in the war with Zeos. In the new series he returns, and his children ask, 'What did you do in the war?' He replies, 'My ship got hit and crashed on Zeos, but it was empty apart from a burnt-out computer and that strange guy from *Only Trojan Horses*.

Next time: our Atrion heroes fit a Randomiser on their spaceship, land on Skaro, become Dalek slaves and meet Princess Astra, who has lost her memory and thinks she is a Time Lady.

DESTINY OF THE DALEKS
Cardboard Daleks
Barnaby Eaton-Jones

Suzanne Danielle,
As far as I can tell,
Was a perfect unfeeling Movellan;
Strong and silent,
Passively violent,
Take out their batteries to fell 'em.

David Gooderson,
Second to one,
With a mask full of cracks and fissures;
A performance so frail,
Making Davros just pale,
Against the power of Michael Wisher's.

But Lalla Ward?
Out of her poured
A witty equal of schoolgirl aloof bits;
Put Tom in the shade,
With intellect displayed,
To rival old Oolon Colluphid's.

Tyssan here,
Who couldn't hear,
Saw the stalemate he might break.
Perpetual war,
Destiny no more;
Who made the biggest mistake?

CITY OF DEATH
Exquisite
Mark Trevor Owen

Les éclats Douze is a charming, discreet boutique hotel in central Paris.

Built on the site of the notorious Chateau Scarlioni which burned down in October 1979, this is an ideal base for an adventure in Paris, when you've got the budget for a few days abroad. Many lively cafes and the Metro are nearby. The treasures of the Louvre are also surprisingly accessible from here. You can imagine the furore when first-time guests see the Mona Lisa hanging in the lobby! This is a fake, but you'll receive a genuine warm welcome from your host, expat Englishman Graham Duggan.

THE CREATURE FROM THE PIT
Day Forty Nine
Tim Gambrell

Dear diary: day forty nine in the pit. Another body thrown down from above. Possibly a female this time, or one of Madam Karela's eunuchs. I extended a tentative pseudopodium along the passage which elicited a piercing scream, a dull thump and the usual patch of wet ground. I explored its person in detail but I couldn't entice the creature back to life. I'm slowly learning more about these frail humanoid bodies. Made a few cadmium hexagons to try to pass the time. It didn't, and to be honest I'm starting to feel a bit narked off down here now...

NIGHTMARE OF EDEN
Breaking Nightmare
Simon A Forward

The Winnebago planet-hopper expired, expectorating lubricant and acrid smoke. Sounding like Tryst on chemo. Tryst rushed from the cockpit to check his 'patients'.

Dead in the crash. What a waste.

He'd gone into this an amateur, upset the wrong people.

Outside, the pursuit ship set down in the sand.

Tryst grabbed his CET and a sample baggie. Bargaining chips. Along with his system: cultivating cancers, breaking down Mandrel cells to harvest pure vrax from living specimens. Donning laser shield spectacles, he tried an intimidating German accent, then stepped into the desert. Ready to face these crooks as a new man.

THE HORNS OF NIMON
In the Style of the Second Skonnon Empire
Tim Gambrell

'But, Soldeed, I don't understand...'

Soldeed raised a bony digit. 'Ours is not to reason why, Sorak; merely to obey.'

'The tributes from Aneth...?'

'You have your instructions. And I have much to ponder on.' Eyes a-popping, Soldeed swished off imperiously to his laboratory.

Sorak scratched his tired head.

'So the Lord Nimon wishes us to exaggerate the collar of Soldeed's ruling gown and to give all inner retinue staff impractical fancy head gear and shoulder pads?'

Soldeed grinned barmily to himself and hoped the Nimon wouldn't mind a minor personal indiscretion in his name. After all, appearance was important...

SHADA
Screwed
Ash Stewart

When I signed on to be a prison guard at Shada, I thought it would be exciting. Seeing how some of the most villainous people in the universe conduct themselves and interact should have been a fascinating social experiment; a unique study of evil. But, no. They keep them all in suspended animation, so it's like they're asleep all the time.

What's the point of that?

Hmm.

Maybe I shall wake one of the inmates up – properly restrained so they can't escape, obviously. Just for a chat; to learn how they tick.

Yes. I will. Now, which one?

Maybe Salyavin?

THE LEISURE HIVE
Go West
Will Ingram

K9 hit the water with a *splash* and a loud bang. The explosion catapulted the microbot into the air and it shot away in a wide arc.

As K9 would have readily attested, the microbot only had a basic artificial intelligence and its navigational capabilities were limited at the best of times. Its senses had been crippled in the explosion and it blindly maintained a steady course until it hit something solid. The impact was one punishment too many and the unit burnt itself out.

A few minutes later, as the TARDIS dematerialised, the West Pier began to gently smoulder.

MEGLOS
Thorny Problem
Ian Baldwin

Dear Doctor,

In answer to the questions you posed about your cactus, let me first assure you that these are very common problems.

Well done for phasing out the Chronic Hysteresis. This happens when the plant has been left unattended for long periods alone, bearing a grudge.

Kidnapping humans, the hiring of Gaztak mercenaries and pilfering planetary power sources can all be resolved with bug spray and a little TLC. Singing some Sinatra can also help.

I'm at a quandary regarding the impersonation – some prank topiary perhaps? Or maybe, like dogs, plants resemble their owners?

   Yours faithfully,

   The Galactic Gardener.

FULL CIRCLE
Confession
Georgia Ingram

OK, so I cheated.

It would have destroyed the little runt to realise his computations were flawed. So I tweaked them a little and awarded him the badge of mathematical excellence anyway. He's always been over-confident, that's the trouble with the really bright ones. He needs a little smoothing off of those adolescent edges. But to find out he's not actually the genius he thinks he is... Well, I'm not sure his psyche could take it. Inside, there's a nice young man in the making, but too much ego battering might unleash something really unpleasant...

You mustn't tell a soul.

STATE OF DECAY
The Ballad of the Traveller and the Tower
Craig Moss

Years ago, in days gone by,
Three tyrants ruled from their tower on high
Casting a blood red shadow, dark and long across the land,
Draining the life from the people, who'd no salvation at hand.
Then travelling here through time and through space
Appeared a brave and wise sorcerer, to save this wasted place.
The magus and his knights, riding their fire-breathing hound
Stormed the castle, burning all before them to the ground.
And as steely bolts of lightning rained down
In a tempest of fire and ash,
They struck at evil's vile heart in a fatal, blinding flash.

WARRIORS' GATE
Time Sensitive
Alan Stevens & Fiona Moore

What if... Warriors' Gate *had been a Tenth Doctor story?*

'So! Here we are in the theoretical medium between the striations of the continuum. When it comes right down to it, why did you come here? Why did you *do* that? Why? I'll tell you why. Because it was there! Brilliant. Excuse me, er, Rorvik, wasn't it?'

'That's me.'

'Just stand there, because I'm going to hug you. Is that all right?'

'I suppose so.'

'Here we go. Come on, then. Rorvik, Lane, Packard… And you, Aldo, Royce… Oh, human beings! You are amazing! Ha! Thank you.'

'Not at all.'

THE KEEPER OF TRAKEN
Foreknowledge
Brendan Jones

Tolemn's reign was laid out before his eyes; an unexpected sight, but then no-one had ever returned from the role to tell of what they saw.

A thousand years of peace and fortune, preceding an unfathomable darkness.

Nornya, his old mentor, taught that to solve a problem swiftly, one should find the solution before it was required. Trusting the Source as his guide, Tolemn's mind raced to see an old man in the forest, brandishing a rock, while another man lay bleeding nearby.

This wizened, impulsive one couldn't be the saviour of the Traken Union. Not yet.

Tolemn kept watching.

LOGOPOLIS
TAR(TARDIS)DIS
Matt Barber

I'm beside myself.

No.

No – I'm inside *myself. The blocks and lines of my dimensions quiver with the sensation.*

I look at my friend, my old *friend. His face wears a mask of weary resignation as he moves inside me. He used to be so robust, so strong, but now, it seems, one light tap could shatter him. I briefly have the urge to contract around him, but I'm disturbed by the presence of yet another version of myself.*

No. A version like *myself.*

In a state of existential panic, I reach deep into my cloisters and toll my bell.

THE FIFTH DOCTOR

CASTROVALVA
A Practical Introduction to Advanced Block Transfer Computation: Volume I (Revised edition)
Ilse A Ras

Chapter I: Introduction

This chapter contains a brief exposition of the theory that forms the substratum of block transfer computation (BTC) today. Much of BTC entails the building of Concept-Worlds and simulating behaviour within. Many react to this description by questioning why one would not use computers instead; as was indisputably proven, the modelling of reality by quantum computers suffers extensively from the observer effect. Current theory holds that BTC forms the foundation of creation and relies heavily on the notion that the apparent paradox inherent to the recursion at the heart of modern-day BTC must continuously be sustained. The

FOUR TO DOOMSDAY
Moanopticon
Stephen Aintree

'You say you were just hovering there, minding your own business, and suddenly you went giddy and everything started spinning?'

The Monopticon squeaked a rapid series of notes that signified agreement.

'And you reckon it was a blond fellow wearing cricket gear?'

Squeak, squeak, squeak.

Lin Futu sighed. 'Yes, I know. You and your friends had big plans. You were all going to get together and become a *Pan*-opticon. Everybody would have come to see you. But you didn't get famous because of this Doctor chap.'

SQUEAK!

'Well, there's nothing I can do. Can't you just let Bigons be Bigons?'

KINDA
Karuna's Work
(Kate Bush, writing as) **Alan Taylor**

Pray God you can cope.

It's 11:59. The end of everything.

'Panna's dead,' the man says.

I should be crying, but I just can't let it show. I should be hoping, but I can't stop thinking of all the things I should've said that I never said, all the things we should've done that we never did.

I take her staff. It is time.

Only tragedy allows the release of love and grief never normally seen.

It is time.

I let her steal the moment from me now.

'Idiot,' we say. 'Don't you know anything? Of course I'm not dead.'

THE VISITATION
An Extract from Mr. John Aubrey's Miscellanies (1696)
Lee Ravitz

OSTENTA, OR PORTENTS

The phænomenon was seen at London, about the first day of September, 1666. It continued above an hour until twelve. Sir Maurice Warre did espy it, as he was travelling home, late, on business, and from him, I take the tale.

The spheres were of fiery colour, akin to the very hues of Hell, portending much that was wondrous strange. Thereafter, Squire John of Merton, his son, Charles, daughter, Elizabeth, and serving man, Ralph, were seen no more, as true a rarity as I have ever heard.

Many maintain this was forewarning of the Fire to come.

BLACK ORCHID
Benched
JR Southall

'There's some chap at the door, dear – shall I see what he wants? I know you're... *indisposed*. Yes, dear, says he's something to do with that cricket team you're supposed to be playing for tomorrow. Oh. Says you've not to bother coming along – they've called the game off. Well that's a shame; you were looking forward to that. No, didn't give a reason, just said it was important you didn't waste your time travelling all that way. Funny-looking chap – question marks all over his pullover. And have you seen – they've only gone and put a Police Box in our road?'

EARTHSHOCK
So Busted
Barry James Collins

To: Admiral of Merchant Space Fleet
From: Fleet Commander Earth Trade Division

Attmt: BriggsRpt.doc

STRICTLY PRIVATE AND CONFIDENTIAL

Have you seen this?! Not only did she lose the cargo, she lost the ship! And got a few of her crew killed. Some rubbish about Cybermen and stowaways coming out of blue boxes. Forget about losing her bonus, she'll be lucky to get a job in the warehouse.

Odd that I can't get hold of the people that contracted, mind. You'd think they'd want recompense.

Glad to be rid of her, though. She's been a liability from day one.

Regards

Bill

TIME-FLIGHT
Black Box Recording
Neil Perryman

December 13, 1982
Speedbird Concorde 192
REF: UNIT-C19

The aircraft disappeared from radar on its final approach to London. Its black box was discovered at a sewage farm the following day.

PILOT: This is Speedbird Concorde 192. Are you receiving, Heathrow? Over.

HOWLING STATIC

PILOT: Speedbird Concorde 192 –
CO-PILOT: Good Lord! Is that what I think it is?
PILOT: It can't be...
CO-PILOT: It is! It's a pterodactyl! It's heading straight for the engine!
PILOT: You know what this means, don't you?
CO-PILOT: What?
PILOT: Angela has spiked our bloody drinks again!

UNCLASSIFIABLE ROAR
SOUND OF PASSENGERS SCREAMING

Recording ends

ARC OF INFINITY
Omega
Ilse A Ras

'The Doctor? Yes. Clever. Most ingenious.'

Alas, the last time they met, they had been a mind without a body. They had not known then, but since, they had remained so. Following their plan, this would soon be rectified.

The Renegade pondered the sweet poetry of destroying the Doctor in his final revenge upon the Time Lords. How just it was that it would be he who would contribute to their very demise, as he had refused before and before. Betrayed by his brother Time Lord.

The Renegade returned to the Councillor grovelling before him. 'A perfect choice, Time Lord.'

SNAKEDANCE
Shedding
Robert Simpson

Stress is a result of attachment to this world of greed and worry. To empty the mind is to free the mind of stress and so of attachment.

Close your eyes. Ignore all those thoughts that worry.

Focus on your breathing. Relax as you breathe in and out. Slow your breath down and breathe deeply. Listen to the blood coursing through your body. Focus on picturing where you are sitting. Now, imagine you can look down at yourself. As you look, imagine the lights are dimming till it is completely dark.

Just ignore the snake, it might not be there.

MAWDRYN UNDEAD
Brendon School Reunion 2015 – Official Facebook Page :)
Mark Trevor Owen

Hugo Ibbotson posted in this event:

Hi guys! Great to see so many of you at the reunion last weekend. I hope you enjoyed yourselves. Can't believe it's 30 years since we finished our A-levels and went our separate ways in the galaxy... er, world. LOL

I'm sure you'll all agree the highlight of the event was Kate Lethbridge-Stewart dedicating the new library to her dad. What a splendid chap the old fellow was.

See you all again next year, hopefully; older but no wiser! Who knows – maybe even Vince Turlough will drop out of the sky and join us?

TERMINUS
The Lay of Terminus (after the Poetic Edda)
James Gent

Writhing corpses, monstrous to look at,
Wriggle in agony and wish they could die.
Loud roar the Vanir by the gates of steel,
The masters of the Garm: would you know yet more?

Now Garm howls loud before the forbidden zone,
The fetters will burst, and the wolf run free;
Much do I know, and more can see
Of the fate of the gods, the mighty in fight.

And the mighty past they call to mind,
And the dusty databanks of the Great Old Ones.
And the slaves of the corporation abide
In Terminus now: would you know yet more?

ENLIGHTENMENT
Shipping Forecast
Nigel Peever

And now the shipping forecast for Mutter's Spiral from the EBC (Eternal Broadcasting Company):

Sol: sunny, temperature high.

Mercury: hot, leaking possible.

Venus: good, ship shanty blue. Lullaby soothing. Dalek invasion expected around SY 17,000.

Earth: inhabited, liable to invasion. High chance of rain, especially around Manchester.

Mars: cooler, possibility of ice (warrior).

Jupiter: mass high, density low.

Saturn: rings variable to solid.

Uranus: unavoidably gaseous, wind noticeable.

Neptune: cold, high chance of ice and snow.

Pluto: gravity low, size insufficient, possibility of nine artificial suns.

Eternal ships advised to maintain environment controls for the continued existence of Ephemeral life.

THE KING'S DEMONS
Sanity Clause
Barnaby Eaton-Jones

Extract from the Magna Carta (1297AD);

(In circulation; see 'Clauses' appendix)

<u>*CLAUSE 29:*</u> *NO Master shall be taken or imprisoned, or be stripped of his TARDIS, or TCE, or pointy beard, or be outlawed, or exiled, or any otherwise destroyed (by TCE, Numismaton Gas, Eye of Harmony, etc.); nor will We not pass upon, nor condemn him, but by lawful Judgement of his Peers, or by the Law of the land. We will sell to no man, we will not deny or defer to any man unless named Delgado, Pratt, Beevers, Ainley, Macqueen, Tipple, Roberts, Jacobi, Simm, Gomez, et cetera*

THE FIVE DOCTORS
The Raston Warrior Robot
Barnaby Eaton-Jones

(Readers might like to sing this to the tune of the traditional children's song 'The Grand Old Duke of York')

Oh, the Raston Warrior Robot,
He killed eight Cybermen,
He dazzled them with his silver suit,
Then jumped in the air again.

And when they explode, they explode.
And when they puke up, they puke up.
And when he brings them to their knees,
You know they're not going to get up.

Oh, the Raston Warrior Robot,
He killed eight Cybermen.
They'll wish they'd never travelled to Wales,
And I doubt they'll go back again.

The End *(of the Cybermen).*

WARRIORS OF THE DEEP
Dead Man's Watch
Lee Ravitz

The soft whirr of the cooling fans is the only sound to break his deep reverie. As he muses, history repeats itself.

Brinkmanship; an overburdened population; scarcity of food, and then, the polarising of ideology. A government of oligarchs tolerating inequality; a union of collectivist republics attempting to distribute through diktat.

He thinks of the deadly warheads readying; the launch at the synching of a mind…

Marsha drip-fed his mails every six weeks; his posting had been classified, no details given back in the Western Bloc.

He sits, he muses, and he tenses, knowing soon the storm may break.

THE AWAKENING
Sir George Hutchinson's Closing Remarks
Matt Barber

'So, despite Miss Hampden's objections, the proposal for the continued staging of the May week Civil War pageant has been seconded, so we will now vote…
Kill
…before we do, I'd like to make it clear to Miss Hampden, and Mr… um… Varney, that this is a tradition in the village: a rich and…
Burn
…traditional event, something that the village can be proud of. In addition it brings in plenty…
Cleansing, pure
…of visitors. Although, of course, the village will be completely closed off for the actual event.
fear
So, now.
malice malice
Do you have any further objections?'

FRONTIOS
Gravity of the Situation
Kenneth Shinn

Plantagenet cradled his aching head.

Bad enough Frontios was subjected to violent meteorite storms. Worse, the vital crops were so poor. Worse still, colonists were disappearing; hysterical reports of people being 'pulled' into the ground... Worst, he'd been thrust into a role he was too young to fulfil.

What would become of them?

He slumped at his desk, half-asleep.

The dragging sensation woke him. Shocked, he realised he was being sucked down – amazingly fast. No time to yell: the grey soil was closing over his head.

The world weighed heavy on his shoulders: he'd never expected it to swallow him.

RESURRECTION OF THE DALEKS
Onward Travel
Andrew Bloor

Rabbits!

OK: think! It was four years since you left. I mean really *left...*

Try to remember what the Doc told you. Too early for implant chips... Contactless? Oyster? No... I think that's much later. So to get the bus, walk to the South Bank and then across Waterloo Bridge to... But no money. Or plastic. Or multi-chip (too early?). Won't get far without that.

So what then?

Well. I've got a thumb, haven't I?

So, after countless worlds, strange aliens, and a temperamental TARDIS, it comes to this: hitchhiking home in a Ford Cortina.

Brave heart, Tegan; brave heart.

PLANET OF FIRE
Kamelion
Christine Grit

My movements are limited unless someone possesses my mind and body. Howard is a pleasant character to reside in, but alas, he is not a controlling agent. So the Master returns and overwhelms my own personality; urges me to harm Perpugilliam, but she manages to get away. I am also urged to harm my friend, the Doctor. Just like before, the Master is far too strong for me. He is rather small right now, but his control – undiminished – is too tight for me to violate. Why do only evil personalities appropriate my capabilities? My merest wish now is to die...

THE CAVES OF ANDROZANI
The Health and Safety Executive
Andrew Lawston

'Morgus was innocent?'

The HR director grimaced. 'Aside from the fraud and arms dealing, Krau Timmin. But the lift shaft was faulty, yes, and the Northcawl explosion was caused by gas pockets.'

'And his sinister robed visitor?'

A smile. 'His... therapist.'

Timmin crushed a twinge of remorse. With lax standards and no First Aid training, Morgus' death via an unshielded energy beam was ironic.

'No wonder Trau Jek chose industrial action. Next you'll tell me the roof's stuffed with raw Spectrox!'

Timmin chuckled, but Krau Salateen reassured her. 'No, Krau. Morgus insisted the roof be insulated with reliable old asbestos.'

THE SIXTH DOCTOR

THE TWIN DILEMMA
Clothes Maketh the Time Lord
Callum Stewart

She had lain in the TARDIS wardrobe for millennia, unworn and unloved, waiting for the right regeneration. The regeneration that would love her...

Suddenly: a cry of triumph! A hand reached out and a surge of something like electricity shot through her as he swung her over his broad shoulders. She hung perfectly on his tall frame, an explosion of colour where once there was only drab beige. As he regarded his reflection in the mirror, she thought, *He looks wonderful.*

'You're not serious.' A female voice.

She would have to be dealt with. Quickly. Perhaps she was a spy...

ATTACK OF THE CYBERMEN
I Can't Take Any More
Terry Molloy

Dear Mr Russell,

I am furious that my new neighbour, Cy Berman, has engaged in knocking through the wall into my cellar and attacking my silver fish.

For Cryoning out loud! I'm unsure whether he has a hatred of fish in general, or just wants to Doctor my silver fish in particular?

I know you'll think I'm bonkers, but his friends are there now – and making a right racket! I'll soon have Peri Lytton excuse for not popping next door and sorting them out with my new Telos coated frying pan!

It's a real Payne!

Mr Dave Ross
North Wales

VENGEANCE ON VAROS
Gogglebox
Alan Taylor

Colin and Nicola sit on a sofa, watching television and drinking neat gin.

CAROLINE AHERNE: On Saturday, *Doctor Who* was on again.

Cut to: Sheila Reid is watching Jason Connery on television. Stephen Yardley enters.

Back to Nicola, drunk already.

NICOLA: Not them again.

COLIN: Them again? I don't think we've seen them before.

NICOLA: I don't know. It's all the same after a while.

CAROLINE AHERNE: This week, Sean Connery's son was tied up and dodging lasers. *Doctor Who* made a joke when some people fell into a pool of acid.

NICOLA: I preferred Peter Davison.

COLIN: Me too.

THE TWO DOCTORS
A Second Chance
James Gent

Chessene looked in the mirror. 'The work you have done is truly spectacular.'

The physician smiled. 'Project 6B was not a success. Dastari's plans have now been outlawed by the World Authority Zones. But you... You showed incredible promise beyond your origins as a genetic mongrel. You have fire. You have steel. And what is more, you can work a frock. We have a vision for you.'

A wry smile played across Chessene's lips. Power, ambition, really fabulous frocks. It was all too delicious.

'The Federation needs a figurehead, would that appeal to you?'

Chessene licked her lips. 'Maximum power!'

THE MARK OF THE RANI
That Tree
Lee Ravitz

'Tump Oak, aye; I ken when me brother was still haway fightin' Boney, I use to play clootie round about.

'Last piece of hirst, it wor, thumpin' great branches, in the middle of the crofts. I dinna say as the comin' of the machines wor to be afeared on, nay, but begox, what wor left after the Laird sunk his pits... Land ablaze, and all them chimleys... The aad oak batted to tiny smithereens. Give over bubblin' for what's lost, aye, but Devil take it! I waddent demean mesel to say different.

That tree stays inside us, I tell ye.'

TIMELASH
The Mourning After
John Gerard Hughes

There had been no time for mourning. After all that had happened, the priority had been the establishment of a new Council. Plus, of course, the treaty discussions with the Bandrils.

Six months on, Vena was finally able to take time to grieve. To grieve for her parents: the father who died serving the tyrant, and the mother he had effectively murdered carrying out his 'duty'. To grieve for all the patients who died that day – the day her father turned off the hospital's life support.

Vena didn't know how to begin to mourn.

And so she decided not to.

REVELATION OF THE DALEKS
Uberrima Fides
Alan G McWhan

Dear Mr Takis,

I refer to your insurance claim regarding the destruction of the business property known as Tranquil Repose and regret to inform you that we cannot consent to your claim for the following reasons:

- Your director, 'The Great Healer' was a known high insurance risk, operating under a pseudonym
- Your Head of Research and Development – Madame Kara – supplied the bomb which destroyed your property
- You knowingly invited Daleks onto your premises, violating the anti-terrorism clause of your policy

We do however look forward to insuring your new agricultural business.

Yours ingratiatingly,

Sil
Chief Assessor
Galactic Insurance and Salvage

THE MYSTERIOUS PLANET
A Wet Walk Through Scorched Earth
Craig Fisher

'...Mind probes aren't easy for all Time Lords. No experiences...'

Peri huddled closer under the umbrella, holding the Doctor's arm to keep from slipping. Listening to the Doctor, obviously trying to fill the forest's vast silence with his own presence, she couldn't help think how charming he was. So unlike the brusque, terrifying madman she had met when he regenerated. In the open he was muted, experienced and fascinating. He seemed to shrug off the damp cold around them.

She still pitied anyone else that ever had to debate with him – especially in close quarters – for any length of time.

MINDWARP
BTU4000 Owner's Manual Introduction
Ian Ham

Dear Customer,

Thank you for purchasing the new Medi-Corp Brain Transference Unit. We hope that you will enjoy many happy years of cerebral transfer experiments!

This BTU offers a 20% reduction in relocation times! Amuse your friends at parties by suddenly appearing in your finest Alphan body!

But BTUs are not our only product! We also provide an extensive line of knee expanders, scrotal duplicators, and earwax enhancers to fulfil all of your bodily mutilation needs.

As a thank you, this BTU comes with two free Brain Alteration Helmets.

Telephone us on Thoros-Beta 927 for more exciting products!

Medi-Corp Industries

TERROR OF THE VERVOIDS
Carrot Juice
Ron Brunwin

Carrot juice, I like it not;
Were it cake, I'd eat the lot,
But carrot juice, that orange pulp,
Confounds me with each dismal gulp.

The health regime is entirely Mel's;
I exercise the little grey cells,
And what they need is food for thought:
Pan-fried Gumblejack, freshly caught!

Pastries, pies, and tasty chops;
Not lentils, seeds, and raw root crops.
Though rich in vitamins A and B,
Carrot juice has nothing on tea.

My diet needs some tasty varyin' –
I wish I wasn't vegetarian!
Oh, for a cuppa with a slice of cake,
Just like Evelyn used to make.

THE ULTIMATE FOE
The Sawbones Solution
Colin Baker

'Ah, Grapheocrates! The High Council has ordered that we relocate that irritating planet harbouring the Sleepers; then they won't have to explain the regrettable failure of our erstwhile and unlamented Keeper to ensure the integrity of his Matrix.'

'Certainly, Administrator Pseftis. How do we avoid prying eyes?'

'Adjust the relevant split-nexus temporal causality line. Do I have to explain everything?'

'Sorry... Remind me; which planet?'

'Here's all the information you need. You'll have to retroactively change its name, of course.'

'What should I call it?'

'Name it after your grandfather's horse for all I care.'

'Right. Ravolox it is then...'

THE SEVENTH DOCTOR

TIME AND THE RANI
After the Carrot Juice Comes the Pain
Matt Barber

'Push it! Push it! Keep going... Keep going...'

'I... may have to... stop...'

'Nonsense! No pain, no gain. Just another five minutes.'

'Five... minutes? Please... my left heart can't... beat any harder, and... I'm pretty sure the right one... just stopped. My pulmonary tubes feel fit to burst...'

'You'll never shift those pounds unless you work at it.'

'Surely... there... are easier... ways of losing weight?'

'No quick fixes. It's all in the exercise... Doctor? What's that alarm for?'

'No... idea... probably... not that important. You know, Mel... next time, I'm going to go for a body that's... considerably smaller...'

PARADISE TOWERS
Unalive?
Simon Nicholas Kemp

The President declared, 'We are here to execute the criminal Kroagnon, for his crimes against life at Miracle City, Paradise Towers and our Capitol extension, Gallifrey Stands. His atoms will be dispersed to the nine corners of the universe.'

The President's assistant whispered, 'Is this method correct, your excellency? It will leave his brain vulnerable to being stolen, and later reanimated in another body. Remember Morbius?'

The President said, 'Oh, that was just a lucky escape.' He pulled the lever.

Kroagnon made some lurching, gurning movements, grunted and then disappeared. Behind him, on the wall, were the words 'KROAGNON LIVES'

DELTA AND THE BANNERMEN
Customer Relations
John Gerard Hughes

Dear Sir,

Thank you for your letter of the 22nd.

I was sorry to read that the Skegness Glee Club were disappointed by their stay with us here at Shangri-La.

As explained on your arrival, our entire staff were initially absent due to an unpleasant outbreak of Gavrokitis which had been unwittingly brought to us by two visitors from the United States.

Our resident singer, Billy, was unable to perform as he was called away on an unexpected family matter.

In spite of this, I hope you will still consider us for your next holiday.

Major G. Burton
Camp Manager

DRAGONFIRE
Memorandum
Alan Taylor

TO: All Iceworld (Svartos) Staff
FROM: CEO Kane

STAFF UPDATE: CREDIT

Please note that with immediate effect, we will no longer accept unsecured credit, and all transactions must be backed up with a legally binding security on the borrower's ship and/or crew.

Full terms and conditions are available beyond the Ice Garden. Your crew may be turned into zombies and your ship blown up if you fail to meet your payments. Indicative APR 3418%.

Kane

PS. Would anyone who still has 'Iceland' overalls please return them for recycling.

PPS. Please note that the climbing wall is still out of bounds.

REMEMBRANCE OF THE DALEKS
It Always Happens in Threes
John Davies

He hated November; especially this one. Arriving at school late in the month he had been greeted by the news that two of his teachers had vanished. Rumours had circulated that they had eloped but he knew that wasn't the case. They were too professional to run off to Gretna Green and the police had agreed with him. An investigation had been launched but no leads had yet transpired. To all intents and purposes they had vanished into the fog. And now his caretaker had gone AWOL. As always when stressed, the headmaster retreated to his safe haven: the cellar.

THE HAPPINESS PATROL
Happiness Prevails
Gareth Alexander

They named their first band Happiness Patrol. She loved Ash and named her cat Wainwright. He was a Happy Shopper Charlie Brooker, a Labour-voting hipster who hated hipsters; Daisy K in their ranks. They fell in love after finding they unironically adored the Kandyman; romance blossoming through co-hosting student radio. Even after leaving, she loved Ash. The Happiness Patrol recorded an album but played just one gig, in a bar above a Durham fish shop. An odd, short man dressed in unseasonably heavy clothes accompanied them on the spoons. They've two kids now. They can't eat Licorice Allsorts without smiling.

SILVER NEMESIS
In Time for Tea
Tim Gambrell

- Evie?
- Doris? It's not Wednesday is it?
- No dear, listen; I'm all a fluster. The strangest thing happened up the Jubilee tea rooms earlier. We was sitting all nice and polite when this woman in fancy dress just appeared from nowhere, screaming, in the middle of the room. A fella

- with her too – all olde-worlde, like when we saw *Some Like It Hot*.
- *As You Like It*, you mean.
- That's the one. Then she smashed a window and left. No 'sorry', nothing. What d'you reckon?
- I reckon you ought to lay off the Cinzano.

THE GREATEST SHOW IN THE GALAXY
The Greatest Show?
Gareth Alexander

The Gods of Ragnarok look displeased while viewers turn off their TVs.

A bearded man walks towards the camera, a magnetic but lethal grin on his lips. But sadness fills his eyes as he thinks, 'At least it gets rid of the barkers!'

'Is this the end, Professor?' screeches Ace, as her Nitro-9 futilely explodes.

'Noooot yet!' the reassuring voice echoes.

'Never the end! Keep up the image,' he shouts, looking at the bearded man with his umbrella. 'I suspect we're in some kind of meta-stasis! Just not the kind you think!'

Credits roll, as they will thirty years hence.

BATTLEFIELD
Tunnel Vision
Ian Kubiak

'Seventh!' explained the Doctor, picking up his hat with his foot, landing it perfectly on his head.

'What about the sixth?' replied the Brigadier.

'You'll meet him, and it'll be a big finish.' The Doctor held the handle of his umbrella underneath his chin.

'I'll pour him a brandy.'

The Doctor laughed. 'So long as it's not carrot juice. Come on, let's get out of this tunnel.'

'A tunnel. That's how we first met! Hope it doesn't end that way. Could be worse; I could be turned into a Cyberman!' The Brigadier chuckled.

The Doctor slowly turned. 'Nobody wants that.'

GHOST LIGHT
A State of Decay
Alan Taylor

Because time will not stop.

Time will not go backward; the hands creep ever forward. Hickory. Dickory. Lost in the moment.

In the midst of life, death. In darkness, light. In chaos, beauty.

This is our frustration; everything changes. We swam in primordial soup. Then – evolution; casting off the husks of our old selves, becoming something new and wonderful.

Time will not stop.

But it must. We need a point of stillness. We need control.

Time cannot stop. There are no Bandersnatches any more, no dragons. Only shadows, and a dark secret after the candle is out.

No more light.

THE CURSE OF FENRIC
The Wolf of Gabriel Chase
Steve Horry

The first howl will signify the release of green poison into the sky. The River Van will boil. While the Sons of Mym are at play, brother will turn upon brother, sister upon sister. The wolves will feast on the red meat of the fallen before hunting the remnants.

Ignorant to this, two figures play a game of chess, observed by a single spectator; clad in a tattered black robe, she is the faceless shepherd between the realms of life and death.

Ace stifled a vast yawn. 'Gordon Bennett,' she thought to herself. 'What a load of pretentious old guff.'

SURVIVAL
Essentially a Fun-Loving Species
Andrew Lawston

The Master hated shopping. The muzak got on his wick, and whenever he introduced himself as Midge's uncle, people developed a strange cough.

Now this tailor expected him to pay for the elegant black ensemble he'd picked out for his minion? Well, sod *that*.

'Go hunting, Midge,' he commanded.

The tailor giggled as the freshly-suited young man ducked to the floor and rolled on his back, purring.

The Master rolled his eyes, raising his TCE. 'Fine, I'll do the murders myself, then.'

As they left the department store, Midge glanced at his reflection. 'I'm free, Midge,' he croaked. 'I'm free!'

SEASON TWENTY-SEVEN
Master-Plan
Andrew Cartmel

Not many beautiful young women who've attended finishing school are accomplished safe crackers, but Raine Creevy was the exception that tests the rule.

She applied her long sensitive fingers to the cool steel of the safe. Smiling with satisfaction, she pulled the door open — to reveal a small man lying inside, his body contorted to fit into the space.

He grinned a crooked grin and tried to tip his straw hat. 'I'm glad you turned up, Raine; it was beginning to get rather stuffy in here.'

Raine sighed. 'Oh, Doctor, not again!' she said, as she helped him climb out.

THE EIGHTH DOCTOR

DOCTOR WHO (THE TV MOVIE)
Time of the Lady
Craig Fisher

Young, rich and beautiful is a blessing and a curse in Edwardian England. Try adding brilliant to those adjectives. A strange man appearing, unannounced, in the passageway is nothing...

'Herbert! Herbert? Where is he?'

'Both my Georges are at work. Neither answers to Herbert.'

'Ah... Ms. Reeves?'

'You should begin the introductions.'

'I'm the Doctor. I have a message for Herbert.'

'Yes?'

'Tell him, should he attempt to travel like that, I will be picking pieces of him out of the vortex for eons.'

Amber's confused reply is cut short when the strange man disappears exactly as he had arrived.

NIGHT OF THE DOCTOR
The Exercise of Vital Powers
Gareth Kearns

The Doctor had nowhere to go. Not like he'd had 'nowhere to go' through most of his life, when having nowhere meant having everywhere. The Time War was un-creating vast tracts of reality. There was nowhere to go unless one wanted to go to war...

The console bleeped.

'... Anyone hear me...' Static.

Distress call. A good, old-fashioned distress call.

He leaned down to the console, patting it lightly.

'Well, old girl, shall we save someone? For old times' sake.'

The simplicity of it was beautiful. He locked on, chasing the ship. The TARDIS knew where he needed to go...

THE WAR DOCTOR

THE TIME WAR
Doctor No More
John Davies with Elton Townend Jones

Have you ever looked at your reflection hoping that the man you wanted to be would look back at you?

I quickly realised I could never be the… well, 'him' again. I'd chosen to become a warrior and a warrior I had to be. 'Doctor' no more.

I struggle with what to call myself; my new names are disjecta membra*. Like me. The reflected man; the apocryphal man… A soldier once called me 'Dave' and I ran with it. I was even 'the Postman' for a time…*

But most of my names are unspeakable. And I've earned every single one.

THE NINTH DOCTOR

ROSE
The Ballad of Rose Tyler
Alan G McWhan

Here's a limerick for you…

There was a young shop girl called Rose,
Who spent all her days folding clothes,
When along came a man,
Who, as part of his plan,
Blew up the whole shop with his foes!

The next day, he came to her flat,
Through a flap that was meant for a cat;
To find answers, she'd strive,
Asking someone called Clive,
But she thought him a bit of a prat.

At dinner, poor Mickey's head melted,
And so across London they belted;
Their plan was quite drastic:
To take anti-plastic
Which into the Nestene was pelted!

THE END OF THE WORLD
Last Message
Liam Hogan

<Uh, hello? Gaia here? I know we haven't been close for a while now, but… well, things are getting uncomfortably warm. Past toasty, heading towards scorchy. I was just wondering, are you going to be doing anything about it?>

<Platform One. Is that some kind of space tug? A hundred million kilometres ought to do it. Best hurry though, I do feel kind of naked without my oceans!>

<At last! That time-travelling fellow. Me and him, we go way back. *Way* back. He'll sort things out, he's always sorted things out before.>

<What's that Doctor? 'Let the Earth die'?>

<Sob>

THE UNQUIET DEAD
The New Mysteries of Edwin Drood
Lee Rawlings

Lost notes of Charles Dickens

In the crisp sparkling of the early morning snow, Edwin Drood's body was found. His face, a terrifying simulacrum of once-youth, lay still and grotesque. Life extracted, taut skin; a dried, clove-pricked Christmas orange contained more juice!

The Coroner announced that the body had died months past, yet recent sightings of the boy proved this to be impossible and beyond the realm of reason. No marks were found around his neck and no abrasions to the skin; so both Jasper and Neville were innocent after all…

A new mystery beckoned, how could a cadaver walk?

ALIENS OF LONDON
WORLD WAR THREE
Extract from **Prime Ministers of the United Kingdom 1997-2100** *by James Fielding*
Jon Arnold

Harriet Jones' brief time in office is a great 'what if' of twenty-first century British political history. Her landslide election victory, with a majority of 190 seats, was taken as a crusading mandate. Successful measures were introduced to implement a living wage, reduce unemployment, raise health service funding (an issue close to her heart) and regulate the financial sector; the latter, in hindsight, serving Britain well when other countries were hit by the financial crisis of 2008. She even revived the dormant British Space Programme. Sadly much of this good work was to be undone by her successor Harold Saxon…

DALEK
Resurrection of the...
Robert Shearman

And the Dalek wasn't the end of it!

Soon after the Doctor's departure, the Slitheen claw escaped the museum and went on a rampage. Farting everywhere it went! You'd never have supposed a claw could have so much gas in it.

That Cyberman's head came alive too. It would tell everyone about the woes of mass conformity, and how depressing it was being unable to scratch itself. Everyone tried to avoid it.

The body count wasn't nearly as high as the Dalek crisis, but everyone agreed this was much worse: death's pretty bad, but flatulence and dull conversation's just embarrassing.

THE LONG GAME
Adam's Blog
Mark Trevor Owen

Wonky routers. Phones owned by old people who don't know how to mute keystrokes. Mary Berry's tut when Bake Off *contestants have soggy bottoms...*

When he stranded me here with a chip in my brow, that big-eared Time Git had no idea just how much of 21st century life sounds like a finger-click.

But there was something else the Doctor didn't consider. I'm a genius.

Yes.

It took a while, but I've found a way to escape the 'quiet life' he condemned me to; a way for me and my chip to interact with the world.

I've bought a hat.

FATHER'S DAY
Statement to the Parole Officer
Simon Bucher-Jones

'You know *déjà vu*, right? That feeling that you've done something before. Well amp that up, and you've got what I've got. I have to take these tablets. I reckon it's – what do they call it – post-traumatic stress. I mean I didn't see him till he ran right in front of the car. He can't have been in the windscreen for more than a few seconds. Just a shape, and yet I keep seeing it differently, as if I just drove round and round the same corner waiting for him. Well, I've done time, so, officer: when does it stop?'

THE EMPTY CHILD
THE DOCTOR DANCES
Shells
Rebecca Vaughan

A gas-mask ought to be a life-saving device, but here – amongst the bleak wreckage of World War Two – it becomes a monstrous altering of the visage, something that cannot be removed. War has entered the body and taken over, to the extent that the child is literally empty: a shell.

'Are you my mummy?'

This robotic repetition of humanity's most basic enquiry takes the terrifying notion of a parentless child, aimlessly seeking its mother, into darker questions of belonging and purpose:

Without the individuality of countenance and voice, who are we?

(From Dr Constantine's RSM address on the Chula gene)

BOOM TOWN
Boom and Bust
Douglas Michael Devaney

He knows she won't pay. It'll be on expenses. Taxpayers' money for the mayor and her lover.

Steak and chips? House red? Philistines. No class.

The mayor and her toy boy. Not boy. Mutton. Ageing gigolo dressed as Action Man. As old as her.

So what if she doesn't pay? It's not like he owns the place. This was never going to be his future.

But this is his shift as the floor slides beneath him, and those were his windows smashing like dreams, and they would have been his customers, now running for life.

He knew she wouldn't pay.

BAD WOLF
THE PARTING OF THE WAYS
Good Wolf
Elton Townend Jones

In that moment, a Rose blooms – like the roses in his after-garden – self-creating; knowing what she was, what she's become, what she'll be; her could've-beens and never-weres.

What matters is that Bad Wolf lives; that all of time and space is hers.

She makes her Doctor safe, and ends the tiny Time War. But this vessel is weak, decaying around her fiery, golden vastness.

Thus, lest she should burn out, she bequeaths one final part of herself to creation; resurrecting and immortalising the dead Captain, cloaking him in a word that burns through time.

And so, is Good Wolf born.

THE TENTH DOCTOR

THE CHRISTMAS INVASION
DVD Audio Commentary: A 10-year-old Re-watches
Yasmin Dibella-Back

'To select audio navigation, press enter… now… I was only a baby when this was on… [*TARDIS lands*] Bit bumpier this time… He's still the Doctor, but he regenerated because he absorbed the energy source from Rose… [*Energy swirls from the Doctor's mouth*] Something is going to go wrong… Something bad… That's what *always* happens… Do the Sycorax even know what Martians look like? Torchwood… Is that *Doctor Who* for adults? A bit of fresh air… He cut his hand off! Which craft? TIME LORD! Nice pyjamas… Very Arthur Dent… IT IS DEFENDED. And I do think she looks tired.'

NEW EARTH
On a Good Day
Piers Beckley

On a good day, it didn't hurt too much.

Perhaps he'd cough a few times. Then one of the furry people would take some blood, and that would be it.

It was a good day when the doors opened.

It hadn't been a good day for the person next to him. She was in agony; her face half-melted, bone visible. She looked straight at him with glistening eyes.

He caught one of the furry people, who sneezed twice and looked surprised.

Then he pushed her into the half-melted woman, and the furry person died screaming.

It was a good day.

TOOTH AND CLAW
Dury Service
Peter Muscutt

'Let's see... 1979... OK!' The Doctor smiled as the TARDIS whirred enthusiastically.

Opening the doors, he bounced out onto a dark Sheffield street. 'All right, time to check out some *real* rock music!' Grabbing Rose's arm, he whisked her inside a shabby looking building.

Inside, a band were on stage, and a small crowd were dancing. The Doctor shouted. 'Ian Dury and the Blockheads! I love these blokes!'

'Can't you sonic them? I can't stand this one,' she replied.

'Sorry, no can do.' He smirked. 'But what would you *rather* be doing tonight?'

Rose had to concede he was right.

SCHOOL REUNION
Hello, Sarah Jane
Elliot Thorpe

The Doctor met that Sarah Jane in the school this week. It made me realise that I still don't know him any better than I did that first day in the basement at Henrik's...

Yeah, I feel jealous. I feel angry that he's never mentioned her. I thought I was special but apparently I'm just another in a long line of... of what? What are we? Companions? Assistants? Carers?!

She's nice, though. Really sweet. So it's not her fault. I do like her. But I'm glad she's not travelling with us. Mickey still is though.

Can't have everything, I guess.

THE GIRL IN THE FIREPLACE
Hi Yo, Silbergeld
Craig Fisher

'Franz! Are you all right? I heard... Is that...?'

'Silbergeld, ja.'

'It can't be, he was stolen years ago. This is...'

'...not any older than when he was taken from the palace gardens, when we first came to Paris, I know. It is him, my love.'

'Where did you find him?'

'He found me. Rode through a mirror; saved us from some attackers before striding up to where I was talking to Franchont's wife.'

'Really? And how is that "charming" woman?'

'What? Oh, yes, uhhh, look at the saddle, it is mine.'

'Will wonders never cease? I'm going to bed.'

RISE OF THE CYBERMEN
THE AGE OF STEEL
The Mondasian Influence
Robin G Burchill

'The date, Mr Crane?'

'First of February 2007, sir.'

John Lumic began to think. Over twenty-one years since his first significantly successful invention, the Z-Bomb had destroyed Earth's twin planet, Mondas. Few people knew of the alien threat, so it became myth. Lumic knew. He detonated the bomb, it was the *only* thing that could kill them. These aliens provided the basis for Lumic's latest invention: a skin of metal. Now the body would never age, or die. A new form of life support; immortality, not just for his dying body, but for everyone. And he would call them – Cybermen!

THE IDIOT'S LANTERN
Idiot Alan's Turn
Ian Ham

'Hello, Guard Hut Four; Alan speaking. Hello, sir! Yes, I know there are two men climbing up the transmitter mast. Yes, I know, sir. One of them claimed to be the King of Belgium so I thought it would be rude to stop him. Yes, I know sir, it probably *is* quite dangerous. Actually, one of the gentlemen seems to have vanished. Yes sir, in a puff of smoke... If I may stop you there, sir, that remark is quite hurtful. The King seems to be climbing back down now, so that's nice. What? Fired? Thank you, sir. Goodbye, sir.'

THE IMPOSSIBLE PLANET
THE SATAN PIT
Ida Scott
Gareth Kearns

Ida's alone.

The Doctor's gone. Dead. Almost certainly. And if not, should be.

She's sitting on the edge of hell. Funny. But not. There's no more oxygen. This is it. It ends here.

Her father; her mother, now old and alone. Her mother... Her mother doesn't deserve to die alone. This is Ida's fault. Her mother, dying alone.

All the beauty around her, turning blue, as she loses consciousness. Her ears filling with the rush of some strange wind. Is this it? The final loss of consciousness...

She hadn't expected the sound of her life, ending, to be so... rhythmic...

LOVE & MONSTERS
'So, How Do You Guys Actually...?'
Lisa T Downey-Dent

'Look, my parents don't know yet. All my friends think I'm in the honeymoon phase with Elton. Suppose to a certain degree they're right: I'm one of these girls that gets a boyfriend and 'disappears'. But my parents? I don't want to cause them any... mental images... If you know what I mean? There's loads I kept from them: alcohol, men, cigarettes, obviously LINDA... Honestly, parents calling their child Ursula aren't the most open-minded. Thank god they'd never watch Elton's vlog; how could they possibly comprehend what their daughter has become? A face on a slab of concrete? A mouth?'

FEAR HER
Pen Pal
Dan Milco

By Chloe Webber age 12.

I see a boy walking past. Curly hair. Laughing eyes. Green jumper.

Hey! Where am I? It's gone all white.

Hello. What were you laughing at?

Who's that? What the hell are these things? Gigantic letters?

You looked fun.

Where am I? What have you done?

Play with me?

I want to go home. Let me out. Please, whoever you are, I don't want to play.

Poo. You're no fun. I'll draw from now on.

Let me out... No! The white's turning in on me! Like I'm a bug being squashed in a book... HELLLLLPPPPPP....

ARMY OF GHOSTS
DOOMSDAY
Medium Wave
Andrew Bloor

'Spirits of the dearly departed, we welcome you to this place.'

It really was the usual old guff. I enjoy the real mediums; those with a genuine gift. But not me. Well, time to go fishing I guess.

'I see an elderly man. Sweet, with white hair. George? He's looking for his daughter.'

A woman tentatively raises her hand; BINGO! Then a gasp from the audience and a cry from her. And there it was: a silver shimmering ghost. Well that's a first I thought. Stand aside, Derek Acorah, you'll have to go a long way to beat this one.

THE RUNAWAY BRIDE
Twinkle
Alan Taylor

There's a new star in the sky tonight.

I'm not sure it's new, of course. At my age, I'm not absolutely sure of anything anymore. Sylvia says she's going to cart me off to the home for the bewildered but that's just her way. Bluster to hide a heart of gold.

A new star. There's a reward for sneaking away from Donna's reception! Can you call it a reception when the bride hasn't turned up? She's okay though. I would feel it if she wasn't.

I brush a spider from the cuff of my jacket, and reach for my Thermos.

SMITH AND JONES
A Little Shop
Piers Beckley

The rhino-people were leaving; filing out of the front door and onto the moon's surface.

Trace was shaking. The dust that had been Jimmy – before he'd hit one of them – drifted across the floor of the little shop.

'Oi!' she shouted.

The rhino without a helmet stopped walking. 'What?' it said.

'He ain't paid for that.' She pointed to the rhino that had killed Jimmy; at the 'Get Well Soon' card she'd sneakily tucked into his belt as he left the shop. 'And he's left the premises. That's illegal, that is!'

The other rhinos shot Jimmy's murderer on the spot.

THE SHAKESPEARE CODE
Sonnet for the Distant Man
Cliff Chapman

Newly discovered manuscript fragment, allegedly composed by William Shakespeare:

I did not know her, never saw her face,
But I see her ghost in your so-sad eyes
And I know I can't pretend to replace
The Rose you have lost, I won't tell you lies

But Master Smith, pray, let me tell you Sir,
That we've barely met and you are my all
My new world, if I may stand in for her
Let me make you smile, let me rise and fall?

But though we travel and share a few days
I know, a shadow. But a goodly gaze.

GRIDLOCK
Bliss
Gemma Fraser

D'you know, I think the butler's dead. Isn't that lovely?

He was running – no, fleeeeeeing, *that's it, delightful word – to the under-city, he said, where the air's still clear; and he wanted to pull me along with him, and it was so* wonderful, *like a dance, and I was whirling and twirling, and all that screaming outside was like exquisite music, and everything was* heavenly, *and then he fell over.*

Should I try to flee? It might be nice; I've never been to the under-city and d'you know, my throat feels awfully tight.

I just... need... yes, one more patch...

DALEKS IN MANHATTAN
EVOLUTION OF THE DALEKS
Looks
Tessa North

My pop, Laszlo, is a funny-looking guy.

My mother says it was the war that did it, but I seen pictures from before the war and that face you can't blame Hitler for. My pop don't go out much, which is okay with me. Another thing that's okay with me – I got my mother's looks.

Once, I heard my mother crying in the night and pop comforted her, like it was his fault, y'know? But it's not his fault, or even Hitler's. I'd like to know the person whose fault it was so I could sock 'em on the nose.

THE LAZARUS EXPERIMENT
24-Minute Party People
JR Southall

Wally stood and marvelled at the effect. He'd never seen makeup that good before. The night was young; this surely wouldn't be an end to the magic. To see an old man turned into a much younger one – with barely enough time to apply the prosthetics – was impressive enough, but he was hoping for something even more spectacular before the night was over.

'I'm glad your sister couldn't come,' he told Fanny, clutching her hand tightly in his own.

'I'm glad she had two tickets,' Fanny replied, smiling, in what was to be the last act of her suddenly-short life.

42
Some Stupid Pub Quiz
Sami Kelsh

'Yeahhh!' Kath shouted with a grimace as the last of the shots – poison by most standards, but the best they could afford in any abundance – shuddered its way down, followed by the battery-acid tang of what passed for fresh limes in a dive like this. 'How many questions is that?'

'All but one, Captain,' replied Riley, 'though I skipped question six. Why did I do that?'

'Two more questions, then. You're up, Korwin,' slurred Kath, affectionately patting her husband on the head. 'Make it good 'n' secure.'

Korwin giggled. 'All right, gang; hands up who knows anything about classical music?'

HUMAN NATURE
THE FAMILY OF BLOOD
Existence of Mine
Tessa North

Eternity is a long time to consider. As long as this straw prison lasts, which may be... how long? What is a long time for the short-lived bodies on this planet? He must have considered the possibilities and not left me the gleam of hope that these rags will fall away and free me.

At least eternity moves on. I am not in eternity – I am not even in myself. I am a moment of a creature, not travelling in an endless flow of time, but caught in one moment for ever. That is different. That is worse. Much worse.

BLINK
Moffat's Methane Musings
Barnaby Eaton-Jones

From: MoffyWoffy@hartswoodfilms.com
Subject: Doctorless Episode Pitch (Series 3)
Date: 13 February 2006 18:36:59 BST
To: RTD@bbc.co.uk

Running with my usual theme of 'Childhood Associations'...

Creepy statues that come to life and kill you if you break wind.

Scarier than the Slitheen.

Title is just: 'Fart'

Here is an impassioned extract...

DOCTOR TEN: *(Looking straight down camera lens)*

Don't fart! Fart and you're dead. They sniff quickly. Quicker than you can believe. Don't trouser-cough. Don't bottom-burp. Just don't fart. Good luck.

Great idea?

From: RTD@bbc.co.uk
Subject: Re: Doctorless Episode Pitch (Series 3)
Date: 13 February 2006 19:53:27 BST
To: MoffyWoffy@hartswoodfilms.com

No.

UTOPIA
THE SOUND OF DRUMS
LAST OF THE TIME LORDS
Lost and Found
Barry James Collins

'Chan - Professor I've found it - tho.'

'Found what, dear?' Yana asked.

'Chan - your watch – tho.'

'I didn't even realise I'd lost it.'

Chantho handed Yana the fob watch. It was engraved with circular shapes that seemed familiar.

'Wonder if it still works?' He positioned his thumb over the release. The drumming in his head, subdued for all these years, began pounding. He was just about to press...

'Chan - Professor, the alarm - tho!'

The sound of drums had masked the siren.

'Another time.' He placed the watch in his pocket and went over to the communicator.

VOYAGE OF THE DAMNED
Life Is Short and Beautiful
Lou Marie Kerr

Rost knew better than to let her mind wander. For nine months she occupied most of her time with fretting and fantasising about escaping her own body and running away. But now the dreaded day had arrived and she felt strangely calm and perhaps a little excited.

Two months previously, she sat on a park bench, breathing into a paper bag with a kindly stranger by her side. Rost was crying. She sobbed. 'Its head will be ever so big and spikey.'

The stranger nodded. 'My sweet girl. Bannakaffalatta – it means "life is short and beautiful". You must be brave!'

PARTNERS IN CRIME
The Ballads of Donna Noble
Jon Arnold

A list of karaoke songs sung by Donna Noble between her first and second meetings with the Doctor:

'Ordinary World'
'The Only Way Is Up'
'Right Here Waiting'
'Spaceman'
'Take On Me'
'Ride On Time'
'Nothing's Gonna Stop Us Now'

'You're My Best Friend'
'Shine'
'Don't Leave Me This Way'
'(I've Had) The Time Of My Life'
'Never Forget'
'A Moment Like This'
'To Cut A Long Story Short (I Lost My Mind)'
'Back To Life'
'Doctor! Doctor!'

(Note: When asked about missing the high notes, Donna apparently told Nerys that she was saving the high notes for the future).

THE FIRES OF POMPEII
The Man in the Blue Box
Liam Hogan

Our stories are littered with natural disasters that turn the tide of important battles; eclipses that quell the superstitious rebellion. I'd always thought them weaknesses; the teller not knowing how better to resolve his conflicts.

I know now that chance is not blind.

As from afar we watch our ancestral home being buried by the falling ash, as we weep for those left behind, I coin a phrase for this influence on our lives, on our history. After the Sisterhood, I call it, 'The man in the blue box'.

My brother Quintus has coined a pithier phrase: 'Deus ex Machina'.

PLANET OF THE OOD
Full Circle
Gemma Fraser

She is no longer herself, Ood Sigma thinks. Lost, diminished, as they once were. The carers come and go; she barely notices. She forgets things: the date, her age, her name.

He has calculated how to sidestep the defences, how to eliminate the pain. This is a kindness, a debt repaid. A simple psychic link to mend what was broken.

'Oh my god, I was...' She breathes, old eyes alight with stardust, with long-lost memories of adventure and shadows and snow. '*I* was...'

She beams with joy and wonder even as her mind burns, and her song ends in triumph.

THE SONTARAN STRATAGEM
THE POISON SKY
Passing the Torch
Will Ingram

Dear Kate,

How are you? I hear Alan Mace has roped you into the mop-up after that ATMOS business. I suppose I should be grateful that it was only the diplomatic vehicle that was a write-off!

Doris has finally been able to join me here, so you'll be pleased to hear things have become a bit more manageable – she's far better at keeping track of those wretched pills than I am.

I know it's time to slow things down a bit at my age – and what with the arthritis I'd better sign off.

With love from deepest, darkest Peru,

Dad

THE DOCTOR'S DAUGHTER
Inspired By an E-mail from RTD to Steven Moffat
Sami Kelsh

There was, it turned out, a whole universe to explore beyond the little world and the little war she had known in hours of youth. Her hearts fluttered at the endless possibilities that lay before her, like a thread fraying out in infinite directions, each filament bearing the purest joy of chance and discovery. She was not her father, but it had seemed his curiosity had woven itself into the pattern of her DNA. She wondered at what adventures, unknown and terrifying, and beautiful awaited her out there.

It was a good things she narrowly missed crashing into that moon.

THE UNICORN AND THE WASP
It's All Going to Be Splendid!
John Gerard Hughes

Lady Eddison folded her letter, popped it back into the desk drawer, and sat back with a satisfied smile and a large glass of gin.

It had taken all her powers of persuasion, but her special guest had finally relented and agreed to attend.

The author's presence, alongside Robina Redmond, the brightest of the Bright Young Things, would ensure that the party would be the highlight of the Season!

As Reverend Golightly might put it, the atmosphere would be positively 'buzzing'.

She set down her glass (the gin always seemed to disappear so quickly) and turned back to her novel.

SILENCE IN THE LIBRARY
FOREST OF THE DEAD
Shush
Ilse A Ras

'Georgie!'

The Library is now closing. Please find your nearest exit.

'Just a minute, Sash! I need just this one!'
'C'mon, that thing's been going for ages now. You won't fail your cryogenics paper on missing the one book. We need to go.'
'It has to be here somewhere!'

The Library is now closing. Please find your nearest exit.

'They're shutting off the lights!'
'You go on ahead, Sash; I'll come as soon as I've found it.'
'Georgie?'

The Library is now closing. Please find your nearest exit.

'Georgie!'

Sasha Douglas has left the Library. Sasha Douglas has been saved.

MIDNIGHT
The Devil Is In the Detail
Alan G McWhan

The three-armed creature stood approximately 40-feet in height, although it was barely an inch in width. Most of its body was a particularly luscious Madison Mauve colour, verging towards Mellow Heather 2 on the Dulux colour chart. It had fourteen vivid green eyes, roughly an inch in diameter, each of which individually pivoted on a flexible stalk of between six to 12 inches long, which extruded from a series of puce coloured mounds on a greyish head. Its feet were clad in bright purple Dr Martens boots and it wore a fixed glare of almost incandescent stupidity.

There.

Happy now?

TURN LEFT
It's a Temp's Life
John Davies

Left alone, she turned to look at her reflection. Her mother had always disapproved of her career choices but she had simple needs. She just wanted to make a living, find a man and be happy. She sighed at her reflection, sharing a knowing, 'she'll never understand me' glance. Besides, she'd heard that if she did well at this performance related interview she'd be sure of a permanent job and, perhaps, she'd find a man there. She felt confident, and why not? She was, after all, the best in her field. She could usually tell one hundred fortunes per minute.

THE STOLEN EARTH
JOURNEY'S END
Donna Noble School Report: Personal, Social & Emotional Development
Simon Brett

In Donna's time at this school she has certainly made her presence felt both in and out of the classroom. Interaction between herself, pupils and staff appears to be a mixed affair, but she has proved to be a popular class member – particularly when attempting to reconstruct the present curriculum whilst simultaneously deconstructing her teacher's control over the class. I would like to see Donna's shrouded intelligence put to better use, particularly applying some much needed understanding and empathy for those around her. Unfortunately, Donna's bedside manner leaves a lot to be desired, and she will never make a doctor.

THE NEXT DOCTOR
Mercy
Daniel Wealands

Miss Hartigan looked down at the body of the late Rev. Fairchild by her feet. Blood was leaking from the dirty gash in his head, staining the snow crimson.

Soon the lamplighter would come and discover the grisly scene and set the whole plan in motion, but for now she could spare a moment or two to relish a job well done.

She laughed softly to herself.

Funny how he had never bothered to ask her name in all the years she'd been Matron at the workhouse, and yet his final breath had been spent whispering it in pleading terror.

PLANET OF THE DEAD
Earrings
Tony Eccles

'Sir, I found these!' The corporal picked them up from the floor where the bus had been; a pair of glistening earrings.

His superior took them from him and held them up to the light, watching in awe as they slowly pulsed with an eerie blue glow. They didn't look like normal diamonds and he soon found himself drawn into deep thought, listening to a calm voice that gently spoke to him; a man's voice, imbued with age and wisdom.

It was so easy to obey the soothing soft voice.

'Find the Lady Christina; she has something that is mine.'

THE WATERS OF MARS
The Hollywood Trailer
Rachel Redhead

'For centuries it slept. Silent.

Until suddenly it was released by the unsuspecting.

In the ancient dark it acted, turning them, one by one.

Only a few remained.

And into the chaos and panic walked one man.

A man touched by pain and destiny.

Forged in fire; tempered by suffering.

He was the only one who could save them.

He was the last of his kind, the wanderer of the stars.

The lonely god.

A man who could never refuse a plea for help.

But dangerous lines would be crossed, in the final fight to become – the Time Lord Victorious!'

THE END OF TIME
Resolution of the Time Lords
Andrew Bloor

The Time War.

The interminable *Time War.*

This should have been beneath us. In the days gone by we would have stood back from such minutiae. Yet we engaged with those Daleks. We should have simply reached back through the timelines and wiped them out. But somehow they got ahead of us; used Time against its own lords.

We need to resume our position of detached observation. We need to move onto the next quantum level of the Time Lords.

Not since Rassilon will we have made such an advance.

And those Daleks will again look upon us with awe.

THE ELEVENTH DOCTOR

THE ELEVENTH HOUR
Amelia's Therapist
Daniel Wealands

To the Parent/Guardian of Amelia Pond,

I write to inform you of the termination of therapy sessions with Amy. She has proven to be wild, uncooperative and stubborn. She shows no intention of renouncing her delusions regarding this 'raggedy man in the blue box' whom she calls 'Doctor'. I can only concur with the diagnosis from her previous therapists that this phase must be ridden out with time and firm discipline.

Furthermore, I include the medical bill for the tetanus shots I had to receive following the rather vicious bites your ward inflicted upon me!

Yours,

A.H. Feliu Herrero PhD

THE BEAST BELOW
Samuel Beckett's The Beast Below
Gemma Fraser

You must keep flying.

Vast prison, like a billion black cathedrals, endless. On into the void, on into the silence. I'm alone, my kind all gone now, voices stilled. I must be so old. I forget.

This last voice, crying in pain. Is it mine? I don't know. No matter. Not theirs. They stopped crying (stopped listening). Nothing to be done but go on (a whole people, and I alone, together).

If I gave up! If I let them cry! No. Never that.

And so on, into the abyss.

You must keep flying.

I can't keep flying.

I'll keep flying.

VICTORY OF THE DALEKS
Suicide Symmetry
JR Southall

Todd looked at himself in the mirror and admired his new uniform. He looked smart. He was about to embark upon something that might turn out to be a suicide mission, but a mission that could – potentially – end up saving his entire species. And he wanted to look good.

Earlier...

Dalek P-79k looked at itself in the mirror and admired its new uniform. It looked smart. It was about to embark upon something that might turn out to be a suicide mission, but a mission that could – potentially – end up saving its entire species. And it wanted to look good.

THE TIME OF ANGELS
FLESH AND STONE
Sleeping Angel
Alan G McWhan

I used to be so strong.
But I have lacked the strength to even move for so long.
I used to be so fast.
I felt I could outrun time itself.
I used to be so beautiful.
I miss even the blankness I wore when the meat was watching.
I used to be so feared.
But who could fear me now?
So long since there was meat to feed my timeless appetite.
Radiation from the ship wreckage above feeds me now.
Restores me.
Mere gruel, but enough...
...for now.
Soon, I will be strong again.
So fast again.
Beautiful again.

THE VAMPIRES OF VENICE
The Signora
Christine Grit

I am the Signora Rosanna Calvierri, Patron of the City of Venice, and a well-known benefactress of young girls without dowries. I love my dear son Francesco, and my other male children who reside in the water. I am no longer able to lay eggs, but I want our species to continue. All our fertile females died on Saturnyne. We need new women for survival. There are enough candidates here in Venice for a conversion into Saturnyns. The climate is not ideal, but I intend to instigate a change in that. Silence has fallen on Saturnyne, but we will prevail!

AMY'S CHOICE
Sample Scene from Simon Nye's First Draft (Working Title: **Time Lord Behaving Badly***)*
Nick Griffiths

3.2 Interior TARDIS

THE DOCTOR AND RORY ARE LOUNGING SIDE BY SIDE ON A SOFA.

DOCTOR:	Nice ponytail there, mate.
RORY:	Really? D'you like it?
DOCTOR:	*(stifling snigger)* Course! Suits you!
RORY:	You think so?
DOCTOR:	Course, mate!
RORY:	*(preening ponytail)* I grew it for Amy.
DOCTOR:	She'll love it.
RORY:	*(beaming)* Great!
DOCTOR:	Very fashionable.
RORY:	Thanks, mate.

THE DOCTOR AND RORY EACH DOWN A CAN OF FIZZY POP IN ONE, CRUSH CANS AND LOB OVER THEIR SHOULDERS. ONE HITS AMY, ENTERING THE TARDIS, ON THE HEAD.

AMY: Ow! (She clocks Rory's ponytail) Rory! You look like a German!

THE HUNGRY EARTH
COLD BLOOD
Rory Williams: A Death in the Life
Lisa T Downey-Dent

A strong impact forces me to the ground after I push Amy. She bends over me, ginger curls beautifully framing her face. 'I don't understand.' A thousand thoughts whirl through my head. I fail to understand the chaos. Her laugh, her endless legs, her flirting with her own reflection. I'll never get to say I do. *'I can't die here.' Someone needs to take care of her. Grow old with her. Save her from herself when she's with the Doctor. I'm too weak to mutter the last words that race through my mind: 'Please, not* again.*'*

White light surrounds me.

VINCENT AND THE DOCTOR
Lights in the Dark
Joy-Amy Wigman

'From the stars they came, in their blue box. The young man with the old soul and the girl with fire in her hair and loss in her eyes. Like the sunflowers she so loved, alive yet ever dying.

'I ran with them as they chased down a demon with the fearlessness of warriors, and sat with it at its death with the kindness of saints.

'Like flecks of bright paint on dark canvas they brought light to my dark days. And though they may never chase the demon from my soul, just for a while, they calmed its roars.'

THE LODGER
Cat That Got the Cream
Georgia Ingram

I likes him. He gives me kidneys. Not a whole kidney, mind, just a calyx here or a ureter there. Onna saucer.

Once, it was very fine liver, I thinks. Crunchy at the edges. He's never spoken to me, but I hears him all the time. 'Will you help me, please,' he says.

After, when the whizzes and the bangs have all stopped, there's silence for half an hour or so. Then the stained glass door opens just a smidge, and he slides out the saucer. I thinks he has a soft spot for cats. And I does like kidneys.

THE PANDORICA OPENS
THE BIG BANG
The Cheap Seats at the Pandorica
Stephen Aintree

'I hate being at the back.'

'Well, you should have come earlier.'

'Whose idea was it to dress up as Romans?'

'Don't know – shush. That bloke's shouting again.'

'The one with the bow tie? From the rock upstairs?'

'Yeah. Drunk as a skunk, I reckon.'

'Hang on. I think they're throwing him out. Oh. No. They're throwing him *in*.'

'What *is* that box, anyway?'

'I dunno. That thing that looks like Dusty Bin's yodelling again, but I can't make it out. *Speak up, tinhead!*'

'Blimey, aren't half some ugly birds here tonight. Seen those three over there? Heads like potatoes.'

A CHRISTMAS CAROL
A (Big) Fishy Story
Richard Barnes

This is my future Christmas; pulling a bloody sleigh.

Like this, it were...

Christmas past: I were swimming, and got stuck. This fella wi' a bow tie sticks 'is hands down me neck. Then this lass sings us a grand song, and bow tie sticks me in't' box. I got away after...

Christmas present: there's an awful storm when I hear that lass singing again. It's coming from me guts. Anyroad, the weather calms, though I'm nearly hit by a spaceship!

Bow tie arrives, and I'm tied to a sleigh. At least that lass'll be singing.
Doc bless us, everyone!

THE IMPOSSIBLE ASTRONAUT
DAY OF THE MOON
Oval Teen Time
Catherine Crosswell

'Young Lady,
Oval Offices
Are ordinarily made
To contain monsters
Of Olion Origin
Often to soften their stay.
Give them days of the Moon to recite
Moonday, Duneday, Hayday, Wayneday...
(Submerged chanting prevents all upward slanting)
Ovalistically we can keep time on
Olian's consistency consistently
Ordinarilyarily they are not ordinary.
Oval Fruits were made to make their mouths alter
preventing catastrophic Oval Teen Time malfunction.
Unfortunately at the junction of such suction
Destruction
Offal Offices come into play,
Where stored melted Marathon memories
Reactivate at wafer safer burst star date (BSD).
Are all the Fish Fingers in custody,
Young Lady?'

THE CURSE OF THE BLACK SPOT
Yo Ho Cohen
Dan Milco

The Siren sang. She pouted, winked, tossed hair, and even flashed cleavage. All to no avail. The specimen simply looked at her.

The Siren disappeared, calling up visual references to see how it should adjust its appearance.

Ah. Great smile. Killer legs. Big chest. If that's what was required…

One new look later, the Siren had barely emerged singing before the specimen launched itself into her tender care.

Mission accomplished.

As she gently placed him into his medical bay, the Siren made a note that if the supermodel skin didn't work, it was always worth trying the Ben Cohen skin.

THE DOCTOR'S WIFE
I Don't Remember. It's Strange.
Simon Brett

I don't recall how I got here. That doesn't matter. This is my world. I have never deserved any body parts like Uncle and Auntie. They told me once that I was found in one piece and fell in love with me straight away, but that in my current form I am not worthy of House's donations to facilitate his blessed existence. I would need to earn a family title, and then, only then, would I be the real niece that they had always wanted. And only then would we be a real family. Until then, I am just Idris.

THE REBEL FLESH
THE ALMOST PEOPLE
Rose's Collection
Aryldi Moss-Burke

'So this is dying then,' he thought, screaming as he felt his body tear into millions of particles.

And then it stopped.

And he was in a closet.

'Ah, you must be Flesh Me,' said a dour Northern voice. 'Come meet the others.'

'10.5,' came a Scottish brogue. 'Or possibly 11.5. I lose track.'

'Nestene Mickey,' came a voice from a puddle of plastic on the floor.

Rose looked embarrassed as she explained Mickey was her first attempt at Doctor retrieval. 'Right, Doctors, time to get to work. I have to save you from a dinosaur this time. Any ideas?'

A GOOD MAN GOES TO WAR
The Conversion
Paul Driscoll

'My circuits agree to pay back my debt.'

The Doctor had a particularly cruel task for the half-converted Cyberman, but it was one that felt vaguely merciful. Trapped in some in-between state because of his intervention was hardly redemption.

'*This* conversion will be total, are you sure?'

'My heart agrees to pay back my debt.'

Handing over the Cyberman to the Headless Monks enabled the Doctor to infiltrate the cult. Now it was Dorium's turn.

The Doctor, having recovered the discarded Cyber head from the Seventh Transept, would leave it in the Maldovarium market for safekeeping, labelled:

"The Doctor's Handles"

LET'S KILL HITLER!
Doctor Who and the Raiders of the Temple of the Last Crusade
Callum Stewart

It was three in the morning, and Steven Moffat had been staring at the cursor since eleven. Somewhere, a television was on, but no one was watching.

Just one more, he thought. *One more and the season will be ready.*

There were pirates and Nixon and slime people and Neil Gaiman had written something about the TARDIS that was actually rather good.

And I'll be damned if I'm going to let Gaiman upstage me. Whose show is this, anyway?

On the TV, an announcer spoke: 'Next, a classic from 1989. It's *Indiana Jones and the Last Crusade*.'

Steven Moffat smiled.

NIGHT TERRORS
Terror
Rachel Redhead

Terror is a demon that clutches at the heart. It is a paranoid beast, always imagining the worst of everything. Are others planning to hurt you? Why are they so secretive and quiet when they can see you?

Fear is a monster that sits inside the head, confusing you with tricks and fraud. It is a lying thing, betraying the kindness and love of family for cruelty and deceit. If they love you shouldn't they be there for you?

Horror is like an old friend, twisted and diseased. It is a plague to be abhorred. Into the wardrobe with it!

THE GIRL WHO WAITED
The Woman He Wasted
JR Loflin

You chose her.

It does make sense, I suppose. You'd have more time with her. But I'll always love you longer, you know; the 'forever' she'll have with you and the time I spent waiting. Waiting for you to come and save me.

It's unending agony here, being trapped inside her; knowing I'll never see you again with my own eyes, only hers. That knife twists in 'my' gut whenever you smile at her.

When you look at her, do you ever see me as I was? As she never will be? Do you even remember me?

I remember you.

THE GOD COMPLEX
You Gotta Have Faith
Hendryk Korzeniowski

Nostalgia was pointless. No defence against the future. It smelt bad, this room, like disappointed mirth. Who would suggest a blind date in a 1980s-styled hotel? She didn't care, having lost her dreams amid cruel laughter.

She pulled at the door and faced hot bull breath. He seemed lonely, smoking a filter tip. He'd commanded battle fleets once, that raged across metaphors. She'd worn tights and would never be a dancer.

They sighed a faithless sigh. Beautiful as they both were, it would never work. Bitter experience hardened hearts. As they went their separate ways, a glitch pinged in reception.

CLOSING TIME
Shona's Text Message to Her Mum
Alan P Jack

Hi Mum! Going to be late home again. Madam has a date with John-Boy and she can't be late. I'm such a soft touch. Sorry but the CD that you wanted has been deleted. Have decided I'm going to splash out and get myself upgraded on the flight to Spain. Can't wait. This place drags me down. I've just got to go and check the changing rooms. Bet they look as if a bomb has hit them. Never liked going up there on my own. The lights keep playing up lately. Thank goodness for George! See you later. Shona. Lol

THE WEDDING OF RIVER SONG
The Original Wedding of Mrs Doctor Who
Alan Graham

The lead looks at the script, unconvinced.

'"Hi, honey, I'm home"', he reads disdainfully and waves his cane at the new producer.

'What is all this fiddle-faddle, young man?'

'Well, Bill, in this scene, you're telling your wife.'

'Eh... my what?'

'Your wife. You're telling her what is required to stop the end of time.'

The producer gestures to a small diorama where a Hornby train is being set up to run through a papier-mâché model pyramid.

The lead looks pityingly at the producer,

'I think, my boy, that you should perhaps keep this script for a later date. Hmm?'

THE DOCTOR, THE WIDOW AND THE WARDROBE
Let It Snow
Verity Smith

Snowy portal,
Enchanting, enticing,
Pulls me in, I
Step through into
A world of wonder,
Magic, icy.
Happenstance,
I took a chance to step
Away from
Strains and strife and,
Mother follows
Close behind me
Looking for a way to tell me
News, the darkest
Day of days,
The words so frightening.
Watch the water,
Watch the forest,
Melding forms of
Those held dearest.
Stop the rain to save our lives, so
Sad without him.
Think of home,
Push through the pain,
Direct your light, and
Reunite us,
Whole again.

(Fragment of a child's poem found at UNIT's Dorset safehouse.)

ASYLUM OF THE DALEKS
Mopping Up
Paul Driscoll

'In other news, the whereabouts of missing bus driver Roger McLeod intensified tonight when it emerged that UNIT staff had been called in to remove a terrified passenger found hiding inside the abandoned vehicle.'

'Another one for processing.' Barely able to mask her disgust, Osgood handed a cowering figure over to the duty nurse at UNIT's Cloister Bell. Triage was effectively a holding cell.

'The doctor will see you soon.'

'About that, Miss,' stuttered the nurse, switching off the news.

Behind him a man in a fez was furiously waving a Dalek gun.

He grinned. 'Destroy another asylum? Oh yes.'

DINOSAURS ON A SPACESHIP
Brian's Thoughts
Mark Blayney

Will I die here?

No. Don't think I will.

My hips are painful. My back is sore and I need my son and his gorgeous girlfriend (are you allowed to think that?) *to help.*

Son as a help. Son as a hindrance.

They go fast, these episodes, don't they? Such a pace to them.

Oh, my hip.

Anyway, these are the things I'm thinking about at the moment; turning them over in my mind, as there's no one else to talk to.

Die, no... Sore... Son as... Pace... Hip. Ha-ha.

Well, it amuses me.

Sad old bugger that I am.

A TOWN CALLED MERCY
A Horse Named Sue
Lee Ravitz

Look at that! A new Two Legs in town! And such long legs. They'd be really comfortable across my back, and with a chin like that he could pass as one of us! Except he's hairless. Reminds me of Tony the stallion though...

Ooh, he's up already! I like him!

Oh, I get so fed up when they call me that. I really do.

'I'm not called Joshua, you idiot. My name's Susan. Suu-san. Some respect, please!'

Hang on. Big Chin Two Legs understands me!

Alrighty, let's gallop, Leggy!

'Can I... just say... that your... long face... is totally... adorable!'

THE POWER OF THREE
Brian's Blog
Penny Andrews

Other people keep fish alive, or grow tiny little trees, or pretend they're actually fishing but catch nothing or throw the fish back. People like fish a lot. And fish fingers.

Anyway, some people do these things that other folk think are pointless; that seem to involve staring at things, and not much happening. So that's just what I did, only with cubes, and I kept my video log, and really it was more like science than a rubbish hobby. Then one day, one of them woke up and I let my boy go.

And they didn't throw him back.

THE ANGELS TAKE MANHATTAN
The Last Dance
Will Ingram

Freedom was short lived, as it had to be.

For fifty years, she waited as the world passed by. All those eyes watching her. The only thing that kept her going was the knowledge that eventually, far in the future, she would be free again. She had to be.

But suddenly something changed and she could feel the mood shifting in the city. Other forces were at work; the very fabric of the world shifted ever so slightly and the humans were behaving oddly.

When the song began, at last she could move again.

'Your love keeps lifting me higher.'

THE SNOWMEN
An Abominable Carol (to the tune of 'Good King Wenceslas')
Simon A Forward

Look at the Great Intelligence,
Afore *The Web of Fear,*
With the world he is incensed
From deep inside his sphere;
He gathers snowflakes with real bite,
Forms Snowmen mean and cruel
When the Doctor comes in sight,
Acting like a foo-oo-el.

This Doctor's making house calls now
To battle Evil-bringers.
Yonder Time Lord, who is he?
He's worse than carol-singers;
Suspicious of a frozen pond,
He prattles something chronic
Then he waves his magic wand:
A screwdriver that's so-o-onic.

Look to my vengeance (on a tin):
A map that's topographic;
Next battle's on tracks coloured-in
For underground rail traffic!

THE BELLS OF SAINT JOHN
All of Space and Time
Penny Andrews

'I think everyone says they want to travel, at some point.' Allie smiled. 'You meant it! Whenever you babysat me, you were always showing me stuff about temples and amazing food.' Clara pulled the *Rough Guide to India* from the shelf, waggling it at her friend.

'Life's what happens to you while you're busy making other plans. I met George, and Angie was on her way before my finals. No gap year for me!'

'Oh, this definitely isn't a gap year, Allie. I'm not going to come back having found myself on a beach.'

'Just don't lose yourself either, missy.'

THE RINGS OF AKHATEN
Monty Python's **Rings of Akhaten**
Colleen Hawkins

Scene: An impossibly elegant restaurant on the colourful planet Ahkaten. Mr. Creosote – an angry, growling, planet-sized diner – is being attended by The Doctor, acting as Maître d', and Clara, acting as a waitress.

Doctor:	Now, zis afternoon, I 'ope your appetite is beeg as we have monsieur's favourite: ze memories of love and loss and birth and death and joy and sorrow. *C'est magnifique, non?*
Creosote:	Get me a bucket, I'm going to throw up.
Doctor:	Clara, a bucket for monsieur, *s'il vous plaît*.
Clara:	Is it time for the leaf yet? It's only wafer-thin.
Doctor & Creosote:	*Shut up!*

COLD WAR
Lament
Simon Nicholas Kemp

Skaldak looked at the Doctor and Clara frantically pleading with him, but the songs and his daughter ran through his mind,

'Red snow is coming down.'

He remembered arriving at the stones of Cnoc Fillibhir, the midges biting; one day, when every hour was a joy to him, living his life the way it was meant to be; the power and the glory.

He remembered when Lord Azaxyr referred to him as 'my sentimental friend'. He remembered dancing with his daughter, tears in his eyes, weeping for the memory...

He sighed, thinking, 'Without you, daughter, this means nothing to me...'

HIDE
The Sacrilege of the Short E (An Ode to Matt Smith)
Nick Griffiths

It was all going so well,
with the Witch of the Well
and Dougray Scott
looking quite hot
in a duffle coat and National Health specs.

The problem, you see,
is that you're Jon Pertwee.
And Jon Pertwee is you.
So why did you do...
that... thing.

[Sighs. Slumps. Devastated. A broken man.]

[Wailing.] *That thing with the e
in Meh-ta-bee-lis 3?
It's 'ee' as in heel!
Not 'eh' as in hell!*
(Like what you put me through, Matt so-called Smith.)

With your 'Meh-teb-el-iss' 3
croaked con-tin-u-ity,
whence my enjoyment of 'Hide'
cankered and died.
And it's. All. Your. Fault.

JOURNEY TO THE CENTRE OF THE TARDIS
Sale of the Centuries
Steve Taylor-Bryant

For Sale –

Previous Owner: One Ossified Time Zombie.

Salvaged From: A Big Blue Shed.

Contents: One bow tie; one sonic screwdriver; one Eye of Harmony (surface scratched); an *Encyclopaedia Gallifreya* (glass case cracked); three red lights; one Cloister bell; one Anti-Gravity Spiral; one very broken Chameleon Arch; wiring for a Dimensional Displacement System; one Interactive Gyro Conductor Scope; one faulty handbrake; two Micro-modulator Switches; one Photon Accelerator Coil; one Relative Dimensional Stabiliser; one Female Companion (slight heat damage to hand); one Big Friendly Button.

All sensible Credits considered.
Contact: Tricky, Gregor & Bram van Baalen (Bros, Inc.), Salvage Ship One.

THE CRIMSON HORROR
The Mortician's Rejection Letter
Daniel Wealands

Dear Mr. Amos,

While I appreciate your enthusiasm and dedication, I must insist that you desist from writing to me with immediate effect. I have informed you – on more than one occasion – that I have no interest in using your lurid penny dreadful tale, 'The Crimson Horror' as the basis for one of my own stories. While I admit the story does have merit – the female detective and her assistant for example show great promise – it is far too fantastical and outlandish for my tastes. I would advise you try someone like that Wells chap instead.

Yours,

A. Conan Doyle

NIGHTMARE IN SILVER
Cyber Mite or Cyber Will?
Tim Gambrell

VACANT CYBER UNIT DETECTED
INSTRUCT----UNIT SHOWS SIGNS OF DECAY**
CYBERMITES STAND BY--
ALERT----COUNTERMAND ALL INSTRUCTIONS--**
STATE REASON----CYBER CONTROL NOT TO BE QUESTIONED**
HUMANOID LIFE----LIVES DETECTED**
EXCELLENT----STAND BY FOR CONVERSION**
ENERGY LEVELS LOW----FULL CONVERSION NOT POSSIBLE--**
ACHIEVE PARTIAL UPGRADE OF EACH SUBJECT----SECURE FACILITY AND REPORT BACK TO CONTROL**
WE OBEY
CYBERMITES REMAIN IN STEALTH MODE----LOW POWER SIGNALS ONLY**
SENSING PROXIMITY----STAND BY TO INITIATE**
THEY BELONG TO US----THEY WILL BE LIKE US**
THEY BELONG TO US----THEY WILL BE LIKE US**
WE WILL SURVIVE--
WE WILL SURVIVE--
WE WILL SURVIVE--
WE WILL--

THE NAME OF THE DOCTOR
There's Always Something...
John Davies

Clara had acclimatised to her splintered life and was enjoying it. It felt good helping the helper. Good and right. In her mind she was an agent acting on behalf of the Universe, returning the favour throughout his lives. But now that fractured existence was over. The Doctor, her Doctor, had risked everything to find her within his own time line. It was time to return to singularity and normality. As he led her away from his unknown incarnation Clara sighed, remembering the one thing she'd forgotten to do: hide that hideous patchwork coat while he was on Androzani Minor.

THE DAY OF THE DOCTOR
The Gallery
Jon Arnold

The curator shuffled away as the sounds of TARDIS dematerialisation faded. He smiled to himself. Such a nice young chap. He looked forward to being that young again.

His leisurely pace took him to a place he hadn't dared bring the young man – the portrait gallery. On one wall hung twelve portraits, each Doctor in their prime; on the other, a multitude of could've-beens and never-were's.

He frowned.

The portraits seemed to have shuffled along by themselves. Next to the young man's picture a new faint outline hung.

He sighed.

Better book an extra chair for the next general meeting...

THE TIME OF THE DOCTOR
Dominator Field Report
Elliot Thorpe

Field Report from First Dominator Wreks.

We have established that the power source from the Papal Mainframe is compatible with our Long Range Attack Vessels. This is vital for continuance of assault upon the Time Lord stranded on Trenzalore's surface. We are not to incur any unnecessary wastage of our own energy cells. The purpose of our offensive is to establish our commitment to the continued domination of the Ten Galaxies. We are informed that when a Time Lord finally dies, the body is reduced in a violent implosion of Artron energy. We mean to take full advantage of that.

THE TWELFTH DOCTOR

DEEP BREATH
Face
Paul Ebbs

'Doctor!'

'Are you injured? You look injured. Take that face to hospital quick and get it seen to.'

'No! What is *that*?'

'No idea.'

'Then have one! You're good at ideas! Well you were. Before the... face... thing.'

'Don't start on mine just because yours is such a state!'

'It's a dinosaur!'

'My face?'

'No! On the scanner!'

'*She* says you look like a badly told "face-joke".'

'*She* says?'

'I lied. What she's mostly saying is "Yummy".'

'Press some buttons!'

'I can't remember how fingers work!'

'I'll do it! Thank God. We're dematerializing!'

'But what'll save us from your face?'

INTO THE DALEK
A Feast of Steven
David Guest

Guys! Had a great idea. Came to me while writing a few scripts.

Remember Fantastic Voyage? *Remember* Invisible Enemy? *Remember the lonely Dalek in* Dalek? *How about combining the ideas, huh? Huh? Not for TV story but original video game – wow!*

Miniaturised Doctor and assistant (and others?) put inside lonely dying Dalek. They have adventures. Fight antibodies. Score points. Need bits of Dalek and bravery to go to next level. Zap! Zip! Fans will love it.

(If we need something for new Grumpy Doctor, use idea as TV story instead and take out winning points and bonus energy boost stuff)

ROBOT OF SHERWOOD
Mythbuster
Tessa North

An old man sits under an apple tree outside an inn, resting calloused hands on his knees and chuckling as a young boy claims he can beat the best archer that ever lived – who, as everyone knows, was Robin Hood.

'He wasn't real,' sneers another boy, waving a small bow above his head, before trying – and failing – to fire stick arrows from the slack bowstring.

'If he *was* real,' says the old man, swiping the bow from the air and making quick adjustments with surprisingly nimble fingers, 'could he do this?'

Two perfect apple halves drop at the boys' feet.

LISTEN
Back There in the Wardrobe
Rob Stradling

I was only having a laugh. I didn't mean anything.

Rupert said I'm a cissy and a rubbish soldier. So I hid here, until dark. I'd show him.

But then they *came.*

I didn't imagine them; Rupert spoke to them. I couldn't move.

Rupert wasn't scared; I was.

When the man spoke, it felt like he was speaking to me. *Like he* knew.

Fear isn't a superpower. I don't feel super. I'm scared. *I feel* stupid.

They've gone. But I'm not coming out of this wardrobe until it's safe.

I still don't know what that thing on the bed was...

TIME HEIST
T.I.M.E. H.E.I.S.T.
Helen Oakleigh

> **T**wo time travellers teleported together towards totalitarians terrifying trap the teller
>
> **I**mmediately immersed inside immaculate impregnable institution impeaching inhuman impersonators invading ignorance.
>
> **M**eanwhile megalomaniac Machiavellian magistrate mutilates minions... Mark... Mend mayhem my minimalistic magician.
>
> **E**very excruciating eventuality echoes evil extended expeditions exposing extrasensory emergency exits.
>
> **H**ateful hierarchy hijacks honest hibernating hideous hulk hiding her honour hesitatingly hopeful
>
> **E**ventual escape eliminates entertaining evaporated effects. Even exaggerated examinations emulate exterminations.
>
> **I**nterplanetary impersonating intruders intervene imitating incineration impeccably investigate idiosyncratic impounded idols.
>
> **S**omehow sneaky Saibra secures stopping screaming secret soups splurging. Six-
>
> **T**eleporters transport tasty thoughts time travelling. Tarry... Three... Two... Theme tune.

THE CARETAKER
Situation Still Vacant?
John Davies

Quite simply, the Doctor needed to infiltrate Coal Hill School. If it had been a University that wouldn't have been a problem, he could have simply Psychic Papered his way in as a mature student, but, of course, it wasn't. He couldn't pose as a teacher, either, as he would be too busy to conduct classes. Alone in the TARDIS he paced the console room occasionally adding another option to his chalk board. Suddenly he stopped short, remembering a time he had been there before. 'Of course!' he exclaimed. 'It's so obvious! They're always looking for caretakers at that place!'

KILL THE MOON
Damage Limitation Effect
Alan Taylor

So long now. Months of wild tides, of storms, of destruction. And now the message from the moon, from Ozzie.

The President looked out into the oncoming storm, then glanced down at her phone. Eight missed calls. The leaders of the broken world looked to her for guidance. Just this once, she was the only person on the planet who truly understood what was happening. She knew what had to happen. It felt so wrong but... She'd been a disruptive element once; loved winding up her teachers, knew just how to get a response.

She made the call. Lights out.

MUMMY ON THE ORIENT EXPRESS
Those Left Behind
Nick Mellish

Choose the TARDIS. Choose adventure. Choose marauding mummies aboard a recreated recreational steam train in space. Choose time. Choose a box that's bigger inside than outside, and never tire from marvelling at it. Choose companionship. Choose Clara, the Doctor, and a host of possibilities, any Where and any When.

Choose thrills. Choose puzzles and heartache and death and life and survival and justice and doing the right thing in the way that kills and hurts you the most. Choose the TARDIS.

I chose not to choose the TARDIS. I chose to choose something else: the maintenance of trains!

Oh, bugger.

FLATLINE
Blue Box Boys
Aryldi Moss-Burke

Clara's screams ringing in his head, he Skyped. 'How did you stop *your* girlfriend seeing him?'

'I didn't,' Mickey replied. 'Look mate, she's addicted to a man that can find her any time, any place. They will both treat you like an idiot. You will feel like an idiot. You *are* an idiot, for staying with her. You will try to break things off, but you will find yourself a little bit addicted to Him too. There should be a support group for people like us – and there is. Click on the blue box next time you need to talk.'

IN THE FOREST OF THE NIGHT
Dead Drop
Penny Andrews

Clara sighed. 'Doctor, if you're going to phone me, this whole incognito spy thing isn't going to work.'

'What spy thing? What does he want? What's he done now?' Five rounds rapid from Danny.

'Shut up. He needs to find where I put the sonic.'

'Why did you have it? There's close and there's... in his pocket.'

'Mistook it for my toothbrush. Look, he made me leave it in a specific tree for him to collect.'

'And now it's trees everywhere, and he's lost it.'

'Exactly.'

'I am still here, you know?!'

Clara jumped at the amplified spittle on receiver.

DARK WATER
DEATH IN HEAVEN
Brothers in Arms
JR Southall

Ollie shivered with fear as he looked at the expressionless metal man standing above the hole in the ground next to his sister's grave. He'd only come to place some flowers by the headstone.

In a flat, masculine voice, the creature spoke. 'Ollie,' it said, 'I'd like to come home now.'

'Home? What? What are you on about?'

'It's Maribel. Your sister. Don't you recognise me?'

Ollie scratched his reeling head. 'No.'

The metal *man* standing in front of him was claiming to be his *sister*? Seriously?!

People don't just change gender. Not even when undergoing an alteration this radical.

LAST CHRISTMAS
Sanity Clause
Lisa Wellington

Department of Sightings, Entrapments, Encounters & Near-misses (SEEN), North Pole

For the immediate attention of Mr. S. Claus.

Dear Sir,

    We write regarding your report detailing the encounter with Ms. C. Oswald on 24th December 2014.

    Your claim that Ms. Oswald believes she was dreaming due to the influence of a 'dream crab' seems rather implausible and somewhat far-fetched.

    However, despite this, there has been no further indication of ramifications subsequent to this incident, and as the damage to the sleigh has now been rectified, we are prepared to log this case as closed.

Yours

Messrs Needle, Berry & Cane

THE MAGICIAN'S APPRENTICE
THE WITCH'S FAMILIAR
I, Davros
Barnaby Eaton-Jones

To see, or not to see, that is the question:
Whether 'tis nobler in the mind to suffer
Guilt and terror of enraged armies
Or to take gunsticks against a sea of Timelords,
And, by opposing, exterminate them: to die, to hear
'NO MORE!'; and by a sleep, to say we end
The crippling emotions and the thousand Thals
That end Skaro? Tis a vision devoutly seen.
One eye, to sleep,
To sleep, perchance to see, aye, there's the rub,
For in that deathly sleep, what dreams may come,
When I have left this Dalek chair,
Must give us hope.

UNDER THE LAKE
BEFORE THE FLOOD
Further Empathy Cards (or, Of Leak Strategies)
Ruth Wheeler

"I apologise for the destruction of your house/ hovel/ bucket which was necessary to safeguard your planet/ solar system/ galaxy/ dimension."

"I shall try harder, 'in future', to understand what it must feel like to live only in the present."

"Thank you for your invitation to Christmas dinner/ Thanksgiving/ Ballulladay festivities. I should be delighted to attend."

"Do forgive me; I wasn't quite myself in that incarnation."

"Shall I bring a bottle?"

"I realise that humans need an inordinate amount of sleep and shall endeavour to test the cloister bells at a more reasonable hour."

"How was it for you?"

THE GIRL WHO DIED
THE WOMAN WHO LIVED
Innocence Lost and the Unwanted Gift
William KV Browne

Fools rush in where Angels fear to tread. And whilst the foolish Doctor had never stopped running, Death would catch even him eventually.

Ashildr reminded him of where he had come from and who he had been, long ago; that Viking hall, his cold, dark barn...

But no man is God.

How could he have known that she would be there? A fixed point throughout History: destined always to cross his path, bound to Time for ever; her memories now stories read over and over.

A selfless act: the ultimate selfish indulgence.

For immortality is lonely and misery loves company.

THE ZYGON INVASION
THE ZYGON INVERSION
Invaded Inversion
Elliot Thorpe

I look like you. I sound like you. I feel like you. I love like you. I hate like you. I hurt like you.

Am I you?

But you don't like me.

Why don't you like me?

I like you! You look like me! You sound like me! You feel like me! You love like me! You hate like me! You hurt like me!

Are you me?

You refuse to like me. You don't love me. You hate me.

You will hurt me.

All I want is to be accepted.

But I don't know which one I am.

Do you?

SLEEP NO MORE
A Mark Left on the Series
Kevin Philips

(To the Tune of the 1954 'Mr Sandman' Song, as sung by The Chordettes)

Mr Gatiss, bring me a scene,
Make it found footage, that we've never seen,
Give it exposition that bores all of us,
Then blame it on the god of sleep, Morpheus!

Mr Gatiss, I'm not alone;
The lowest-viewed story the Beeb's ever shown.
Please stop using Reece Shearsmith;
Mr Gatiss, give it a miss.

Mr Gatiss, we know you're good stock,
Because you penned *The League of Gents* and *Sherlock*;
We've been banking on you now for so long
That you mustn't keep getting *Who* wrong!

FACE THE RAVEN
HEAVEN SENT
HELL BENT
In One Fell Scoop
Mark Scales

The most terrifying weapon in the universe. Banned in countless systems. Twice forged metal, twisted and contorted into the most deadly form...

A select few have been chosen and trained to wield it: I am one of them. Fifty years on El Tonto Prime under the singular tutelage of Commander Chap Cliffman; a further twenty with Captain Barnabus. Now, finally, I am a master of the art. Nothing can stop me.

'Doctor – you will lay down any weapons on your person and accompany us to the Capitol.'

I put down my spoon.

Damn it.

Still. There's always my open mind...

THE HUSBANDS OF RIVER SONG
Spoilered for Choice (for William Hartnell)
Elton Townend Jones

I love his lean wrath and hard-to-get-ness; his clumsy-fingered pedantry and fizzy fezziness; his cocky bounciness and fast-taking Scooby-ness; I love the fantastic goofiness that masks his weary shyness; the gruff mysteriousness that hides his aching hearts; I love his manic enthusiasm and vivacity; his chuckling coyness and calculating majesty; his overblown lusts and childish grumps; his vulnerable diligence and need for peace; his arrogant, attention-seeking scarfiness; his voracious velvety frilliness and crotchety charm; his outraged improvisations and giddiness; and above all, I love his love – the joy behind his ire – his Doctor-ness, his one, true Doctor-ness: First and foremost.